DATE DUE

S OCT 25 1979	F NOV 1 8 1997	
G APR 8 1980		
4 OCT 8 1982		
4 NOV 3 0 1982		
M JUL 3 1984		
M JAN 1 1 1986		
M FEB 1 1986		
JAN 3 0 1988		
MAR 1 6 1988		
JUN 2 8 1988		
T MAY 1 2 1992		
T AUG 8 1992		
AUG 2 5 1992		
F AUG 1 8 1997		
F SEP 2 3 1997		

Eden
    An afternoon walk   (Large type)

SSG 14/92

AN AFTERNOON WALK

Dorothy Eden

G.K.HALL & CO.

 Boston, Massachusetts

1972

Library of Congress Cataloging in Publication Data

Eden, Dorothy, 1912–
  An afternoon walk.

  Large print ed.
  I. Title.
[PZ3.E2129Af5] [PR6055.D4] 823'.9'14 72-8983
ISBN 0-8161-6057-0

Copyright © 1971 by Dorothy Eden

Published in Large Print by arrangement
with Coward, McCann & Geoghegan, Inc.

Set in Photon 18 pt Times Roman

Chapter 1

Ella hadn't meant to walk so far. But the afternoon was so beautiful, so hot and hazy and windless, with the fields full of tall waving grass, white daisies and red poppies, that she had not called to Kitty to stop.

Kitty, in her short yellow dress, danced ahead as lightly as the butterfly she hoped to snare in her net. She waved the net with such eager abandon, however, whenever she saw a butterfly alight on a twig or a flower, that it was gone, floating into the air like a scrap of charred paper, long before she reached it.

Then her enormous expressive eyes were turned on Ella in chagrin, and she complained that butterflies would never stay still, it wasn't as if she intended to *hurt* them.

1

Kitty, it was well known, would not have hurt a fly, or an ant, or a worm, or the most humble of living creatures. Kitty was the one who was always begging for damaged things to be made whole. A butterfly in her net now would only be for the purpose of studying with wonder its colors, the iridescent sheen of a red emperor or a clouded yellow. A white cabbage moth would be better than nothing.

Ella remembered that when she had been a child it had been no surprise to find a purple emperor, a clouded yellow and a peacock all in one afternoon, Now, like larks and nightingales, butterflies were disappearing. It was sad.

She longed for Kitty to have all the pleasures she had had, and for this reason, when Kitty saw the vague shape of the ruined house in the distance, standing behind its screen of oaks and rhododendrons, like an image in a cloudy mirror, she didn't insist that they go no farther. They had come a long way, and there would be the walk back, which Kitty's six-year-old legs would find exhausting.

Besides, the house looked intriguing. She

hadn't known it was there. They could rest in the shade of a tree before tentatively exploring the garden, and perhaps the house itself. One imagined by the blank look of the windows that the place would be empty. It was a long way from the main road, and even this track across the fields seemed miles from the comfortable suburbia where they lived. Looking back, Ella could see only a low shimmer of roofs in the distance. They were deep in the country. They had never come so far before, simply because there had never been such a warm dreamlike day, since she and Max had lived in Collingham. There had been rain and wind and dripping trees and flattened wet grass. They had stayed in the confines of the garden and the tidy streets. But suddenly, in mid-July, summer had come, and the whole vista was changed. They had horizons beyond the rooftops of Collingham. Today, she and Kitty were explorers.

What fun to have found a ruined house to investigate. Perhaps the overgrown garden, undisturbed by power mowers and fertilizers, would be a haven for all the butterflies she remembered. It would be like turning her life back and becoming a child again.

She wore a sleeveless cotton dress and sandals, and her blond hair hung loose, like Kitty's. She felt blithe and carefree, as she hadn't done since she had lost the baby, certainly as she never seemed to feel when Max was home and his tensions pressed on her.

But what better recipe for being blithe and carefree than walking in the summer fields with one's beloved daughter on a hot still afternoon?

She and Kitty peered through a rusted iron gate down a tangled dark weedy path. Kitty raised apprehensive eyes. Even Ella had the first stirring of rather enjoyable unease.

"Who lives in there?" Kitty whispered, as if the owner were lurking behind one of the dark tree trunks, listening.

"I shouldn't think anybody does. I expect there's a NO TRESPASSING sign on the front gate. But this is the back gate and it doesn't tell us not to go in."

Kitty's hand slid into Ella's and held on firmly. The gate gave a loud groan as Ella pushed it open. They tiptoed up the shaded path until a curve brought them in sight of the garden bathed in the hot hazy sunlight, and alive with the white cabbage moths, and buzzing bees. Beyond its neglected lawns and flower beds stood the old house. The uncurtained, uncleaned windows had a blind look. The house was faded, paintless, dilapidated. One corner of the roof was falling in, the slats beneath vanished tiles like exposed bones. Yet the house didn't look so old, no more than a hundred or a hundred and twenty years. It might have been a Victorian vicarage, except that there was no church near. Or perhaps it had been a rather splendid farmhouse, only where were the stables and cow sheds?

There was the hum of bees, and the cawing of rooks in a nearby elm, and a strong scent of stock and sun-warmed wallflowers, and wild flowering currant.

Kitty was enchanted.

"Mummy, it's a real garden."

The overgrown plants and weeds came nearly to Kitty's head. Was this what she had always imagined a garden should be, rather than the neat oblong that Max brushed and tailored every weekend?

"There's millions of butterflies, Mummy. Oh, look, I've caught one!"

It was only one of the common pesty white ones, but it was Kitty's first catch. She examined it eagerly, then shuddered and threw net and all on the ground. "Ugh, it's got horrid wriggly legs. It's like a caterpillar. I thought butterflies only had wings."

Kitty's first lesson in nonperfection?

"They're caterpillars before they're butterflies, darling. Look, here's a dear little cobbled path. I think it leads up to the house. Shall we follow it?"

"Supposing there's someone at home." Kitty's voice was again a whisper.

"Nobody's lived here for years, by the look of it. I wonder who did use to live here."

"Yes, who? Tell me."

"I don't know. A mother and a father and several children, I expect. And a nanny and an under-nanny and a cook and three housemaids and a boots' boy, and a gardener."

They were close to the house now. The

path led to a terrace that ran past long low windows, and Ella, pressing her nose against the dusty glass, could make out a large room with two fireplaces, peeling crimson wallpaper, and a floor littered with fallen plaster and soot.

Kitty rubbed a bit of the glass clean, making a porthole through which to look.

"What an enormous room!"

"I expect it was the drawing room."

"Is that where the mother and the father and the children would sit?"

"The mother and father, certainly. The children would be brought in by their nanny when they were clean and on their best behavior. Their mother would read to them out of a book called *Ministering Angels* and then kiss them good night."

"How many children?" Kitty demanded.

"Oh, I should think six or seven."

"Would their father kiss them, too?"

"Of course."

"Before he went to the office?"

"He may not have had an office. I think he was probably a gentleman of independent means. That's why he built this house away from town and yet not too far away. They would have a carriage and go shopping and visiting."

"Look, Mummy!" Kitty squealed. "One of the children was very naughty. She wrote on the window. What does it say?"

Ella pored over the thin scratching. She had to read the letters backward. What was the name? Suddenly it seemed vital to know. She felt excited. Her make-believe was becoming reality.

"Edith," she pronounced triumphantly.

"Who was Edith?"

"The eldest daughter," Ella said with certainty. "The rebel. She thought living away out here was dull. She wanted to put on her best crinoline and go dancing every night."

"Crinoline?" said Kitty, testing a new word.

"That's a skirt that hung on a wire frame and looked like an enormous lampshade. Very becoming for young ladies with slim waists but also very uncomfortable. You had to have very wide chairs and wide doorways."

"Then what happened to Edith when she put on her crinoline? Did she run away?"

"I don't know. I expect she married a suitable husband."

What was a suitable husband? Someone who was a good provider, who telephoned nightly when on one of his frequent trips abroad, and always brought back gifts for his wife and child, who didn't have affairs with other women (as far as Ella knew, and she was sure she would know if Max did), who was personable and hardworking and ambitious. If anything, too ambitious, too conscious of money as a status symbol, though one admitted it was nice in other more practical ways. Would that kind of husband have satisfied Edith? Not the money part, perhaps. Money to her would have been a vulgar subject.

"Tell me more, Mummy," Kitty demanded.

Ella laughed. "Darling, I'm only making it up."

But she wasn't, entirely. The room, dusky behind the grimy windows, seemed peopled with the family she had created in her mind. The hot dreamy afternoon, the wild garden with its vivid scents, the lonely silent house, were making so deep an impression on her that she wanted to go on wishing herself into the past, into being Edith, the rebel, who borrowed her mother's diamond ring to cut her name in the windowpane, who married a devoted husband and watched Queen Victoria's jubilee procession.

"Mummy, can I pick some flowers?"

Ella looked at the tangle of roses and foxgloves and purple willow herb and perennial phlox and marigolds and marguerite daisies. Who had last picked flowers in this garden? In a wooden basket, with the gardener looking on disapprovingly — as Max looked when she begged for some carnations or delphiniums from his immaculate borders.

"I expect you can, darling. Be careful of the thorns."

She couldn't tear herself away from the sun-baked terrace and the closed windows. She went to look in the next room where a piece of glass was broken out of the window and the dark musty smell of a closed forgotten house came out. Dust, birds' nests, mice. This must have been the ballroom, but now the floor had gaping holes as if the damp had come up and everything was rotted.

There couldn't have been anybody here for years. One wondered why this house had been left to die. Litigation over a will, perhaps. Some sinister happening in the past? A road being planned through the garden and smack through the middle of the house? Or merely bad foundations that would not warrant the expense of renovation?

"Oh, Mummy, there are prickles!" Kitty wailed.

Ella turned vaguely to look at Kitty's small figure, then back to the empty room and fancied she saw something move. Not a rat. Something larger and shadowy in the dark passage beyond the open door.

She pressed her nose eagerly against the pane, then stiffened and gasped as the scream rang out.

Where did it come from? Somewhere in the invisible upper part of the house? A spasm of pure terror had seized Ella. She had to will herself to step backward to look upward at the rows of silent windows.

At the exact moment that she raised her eyes a white form burst from an attic window and floated over the garden, wings outspread. The window hung open after its departure.

Kitty was flying up the path, her face full of alarm.

"What was that, Mummy? That noise?"

"Only a screech owl, darling. Look, there it goes."

Kitty clung to Ella, her small hands damp with perspiration.

"It makes a horrid noise."

"Yes, doesn't it? I've always thought owls are uncanny things. Have you got enough flowers? I'll help you. Then we must go or Daddy will be home before us."

She fancied, as she tugged marigolds out of the clinging weeds, that she heard a more mundane sound than the cry of a screech owl, the sound of a car starting. But she wasn't sure. The rooks were cawing and there was a tractor put-putting in the distance. Walking to the side of the house to look, it seemed to her that there was a faint cloud of dust hanging over the drive, but on reflection she decided it was only the heat haze. She had meant to explore the front as well as the back of the house, but now thought better of it. She was still affected by that strange eerie feeling, and besides, they had lingered long enough. They would come back again another day. She would bring a picnic lunch and they would eat it on the terrace, and she would tell Kitty more about Edith and her brothers and sisters. Perhaps they had had a sadistic Victorian father who occasionally beat them. Or his wife. . . . But she, poor thing, would have to suppress her screams in case the servants heard.

It was a haunted house, and Ella, always acutely susceptible to atmosphere, had picked up its aura. She mustn't frighten Kitty. Max would laugh at her when she told him the events of their afternoon walk. He would say it was her subconscious desire for gracious living that had made her like the old house.

But how would he explain the instinctive terror, not entirely dissolved even when one knew its innocent cause?

It must have been that lingering uneasiness that made her imagine someone followed her and Kitty through the dark shrubbery. She thought she heard a twig snap, and when she looked back a branch swayed very slightly. Had a bird just alighted on it? There was no other sign of movement.

It seemed as if the sun had lost a little of its brightness when she and Kitty emerged into the open field and the safe path for home.

Safe? Why had she thought that, as if they had been in danger?

The haze had deepened, the town was a smoky blur in the distance. Looking back again compulsively to the house, shadowy and sad in its nest of greenery, she could see the attic window still hanging open after the owl's precipitate flight.

What, she wondered, had disturbed the bird?

Well, one of a dozen things. Herself calling to Kitty, a stray cat, a stair creaking as stairs in old houses did, or even a nest of fledglings somewhere who would be demanding attention. It was nothing to concern her and Kitty. Their little adventure was over.

Except that she couldn't get rid of the uncanny feeling that they were being followed. The path ran along the side of the hedge, thick with cow parsley, brambles and foxgloves. In some places it was higher than her head. Someone could easily be concealed on the other side.

Nobody was, of course. For who would want to follow a little girl with a butterfly net and a woman with her arms full of a tangled mass of flowers, and never make his presence known? What would be the point?

All the same, now that Kitty was going to school, she must warn her about strange men. It was so sad, having to spoil a child's innocence. First there had been the promised baby that had never come, and now this necessary emphasis on the fact that everybody Kitty met was not her friend. Like the pretty silken butterfly with the ugly crawly feet.

That is life, Kitty, sad to say.

Chapter 2

Max telephoned from the airport, and said he would be home in half an hour. He was going to treat himself to a taxi. He couldn't wait for the day, Ella knew, when a company car would be sent to meet him after his trips abroad. He had secret hopes that that was going to happen quite soon. The export manager was retiring and applications for the job were open to Max and one or two other candidates. Although Max was the lowest in seniority he was not only hopeful but confident of getting it.

His aura of confidence was the thing that made him so successful a salesman. He managed to make his product an offshoot of his own sincerity and honesty. People trusted him. He usually came back from a trip abroad with a full order book.

If he got the job of export manager he wouldn't need to travel so much, and when he did it would be done with more prestige. A chauffeur-driven car to take him to and from the airport, first-class air travel and first-class restaurants and hotels. It would all suit his taste for luxury.

Undoubtedly it would mean that they would have to get a bigger house, in a snob area, such as one of those new expensive housing estates outside Esher or Weybridge. Ella would have to entertain, too. That was inevitable. The only reason Max hadn't insisted on small smart dinner parties before this was because he was now a little ashamed of their completely ordinary, tasteless house. He hadn't been when they had moved to Collingham. He had thought it a suitable temporary house for a businessman on his way up. But since it was temporary he hadn't wanted Ella to spend money on it, and anyway she had been defeated by it from the beginning. As a consequence she hadn't persuaded him to let her do interesting things with the lounge-dining room, or the ugly staircase leading to the completely characterless bedrooms on

17

the second floor.

One would have had to begin by pulling out the horrible brick fireplace, and that Max would have regarded as really a foolish waste of money. He quite liked it. Neither did he mind the rather coy archway dividing the sitting part from the dining part of the room. At least he hadn't done so at the beginning. Now he was talking loftily of cocktail bars and terraces. He had outgrown the house.

But he had not outgrown his wife. He had been far more farseeing when marrying than when investing in property. Ella, he was very well aware, was a class above him. Indeed, her impoverished but proud country family hadn't liked the idea of her marrying him at all. He frequently complained that they were still damned snooty toward him. But Ella, doing everything wholeheartedly, had flung herself into his arms and into marriage, and, with her looks, which always attracted attention (they were delicate and a little fey, not pretty, but distinctly unusual), and her natural social sense, Max had known that she would fit beautifully into the position of an executive's wife, even that of wife to the managing director. As far as Max's ambitions went, nothing was impossible.

Ella had always known these things about her husband. He had made no secret of them. Rather than repelling her, she had been fascinated by his drive, his enthusiasm, even his periods of acute tension when he was extremely difficult to live with. His dark good looks had excited her very much. She thought that he was twice the man her slow-drawling correctly mannered brothers were, and why was it vulgar to talk of money when money was the uppermost thought in most people's minds, and export was being preached like a new religion?

She thought it would be amusing to be a a managing director's wife.

Six years later she knew she had made a mistake about that. It would be deadly dull. Boring, stultifying, hypocritical. Even to be the wife of the export manager would demand qualities which she simply hadn't got, and moreover didn't want to have. She would have to pretend all the time.

Fortunately she was quite good at pretending. She would do so for Max's sake. Because she still loved him. She still waited eagerly for his return from his trips, hurrying to have the house clean, flowers on the table, a good meal prepared, and herself and Kitty freshly bathed and in their prettiest dresses. Max had a strong driving personality, and even in his bad moods he made the house come to life.

It was lucky today that they had found all those flowers in the garden of the old house. Now Ella didn't need to plunder the garden, because she swore Max had counted every bloom and every bud before he went away, and would know exactly where she had cut the roses or the peonies.

That neat garden was his pride and his private therapy. It seemed as if for him no flower would dare not to bloom to the best of its ability. The trouble was that the garden was as lacking in a natural freedom and exuberance as a well-kept filing cabinet. It was like a healthy balance sheet. The summer flowers were planted so that they would bloom at exactly the time the daffodils and tulips were fading. The beds must never look impoverished or bankrupt. It was doubtful if a slug or an aphid had ever ventured through the garden gate. The birds using the birdbath had the glossiest of feathers.

Arranging her flowers in an overflowing colorful mass in an old soup tureen, Ella thought fondly of Edith's garden. A bit of broken statuary covered with ivy, some intractable wild climbing roses, some strawberry plants among the polyanthus — that was what a garden needed.

But theirs was as well ordered as Max's life and his plans for the future. It was planned to be immune to any disaster, except something cataclysmic such as a typhoon or a direct hit by a thunderbolt.

"Kitty," Ella called. "You've left your dolls' pram on the lawn. Go and put it away before Daddy comes. You know he doesn't like the garden to be untidy."

Kitty went obediently, but grumbling to herself. She returned, dragging the dilapidated perambulator full to overflowing with her shabby but much-loved dolls, her family as she called them.

"I don't expect Daddy would care for our garden, would he, Mummy?"

"Our garden?"

"The one we found today."

"It isn't really ours, darling."

"It is, because we discovered it. We'll go there again, won't we? It was sort of scary, but I liked it. I wish I had six brothers and sisters like Edith had. When will Daddy be home?"

"Any minute."

Ella washed lettuce leaves and radishes and spring onions. It was too hot for anything but a salad and cold ham and hard-boiled eggs. A chilled melon to start. She wasn't concentrating. She kept looking out of the window across the fields to the clump of trees, far off and dark on the horizon. She was like Kitty, a little bemused by that secret garden and the empty house. It must be the heat that was making them both dreamy and imaginative.

The chiming doorbell (a horror that Max found amusing) rang, and there was Max on the doorstep. He looked neat and well groomed as always, and only the slightest bit travel-stained. His dark good looks gave Ella her habitual feeling of pleasure. She was sure that even an emergency landing and a hasty exit down the escape chute would still leave him without a hair out of place, or a speck of dirt on his shining white shirt.

No long-haired fashion or psychedelic shirts or ties for Max. He was like his garden, spick-and-span and smelling of the right things. If ever there were a campaign against dishevelment, Max would lead it.

He stooped to kiss Ella briefly.

"God, I'm tired and filthy. London Airport was like the tropics. How long have you had this hot weather?"

"Since yesterday. Kitty and I — "

"Where's Kitty? Isn't she coming to welcome me home?"

Kitty appeared obediently and gave Max a prim kiss, but wriggled out of his embrace in a moment. She was not a demonstrative child. Max sometimes complained about this, not realizing, as Ella did, the intense passions shut in Kitty's little breast. Ella only knew because she was the same herself.

Of course Max knew all about her passions, even if he found them a little inconvenient when they obtruded on his business preoccupation.

"I've got some things in my bag," Max

was saying. "But wait until I've had a shower, eh?"

Kitty stood back tentatively.

"Did you remember to bring something for Sam, Daddy?"

"Sam?"

Ella saw Kitty's face and said quickly, "You must remember Sam, darling. He's Kitty's best friend."

"I told you, Daddy," said Kitty.

"Oh, yes, yes. Sam. Well, as a matter of fact — now look here, hasn't he a father to get things for him?"

"Not one who goes abroad," Kitty said. "It isn't the same thing, just shopping in Collingham."

Max frowned, then laughed.

"I quite agree. Next time I promise to remember Sam. Ella, we seem to have an expensive and sophisticated daughter. She prefers foreign goods. Bad for the national economy. Look, I must get that shower. Any calls from the office?"

"No."

"Good. I can relax until tomorrow morning. I've had a great trip. Broken records. How about a bottle of vino with supper? Haven't we got some of that Chianti left?"

He was in a good mood. The tension lines were absent from his mouth. Ella allowed herself a small sigh of relief. She knew what her gift would be. A bottle of French perfume, duty-free. She had a drawerful of small elaborately packaged bottles. Max never seemed to notice that she seldom wore the kind of perfume he brought her. It was too heavy and cloying. Not her at all.

If a man didn't understand the kind of perfume that suited his wife, did he understand his wife? A moot point. Not one to get upset about, after six years of marriage. The significant thing was the gift, not whether she liked it. He remembered her. That was what mattered. Not like Kitty's forgotten Sam. Funny little Kitty and her ardent devotions, of which her father was also unaware.

"Well, what have you two girls been doing on this lovely summer day?" Max asked at supper.

"We found a big empty house and garden," Kitty said excitedly. "Look, we picked all those flowers out of the garden."

"A lot of weeds," Max said good-humoredly. "I wondered where they came from."

"It was an untidy garden," Kitty said explicitly. "Not like ours. And an owl screamed in the house."

Max looked at Ella. Ella explained, "We went for a long walk looking for butterflies. We found this deserted house. Isn't it strange how such a place could be allowed to fall into wrack and ruin? With the housing shortage you'd think someone would be glad to live there. There'd be room for several families."

"Where is it?" Max asked, with only perfunctory interest.

"Across the fields. I should think about two miles from here."

"Don't know it. I expect it's scheduled for demolition. Perhaps there's a road going through there."

"It's a *haunted* house," Kitty said, enjoying the importance of the word. "Once a mother and father and lots of children lived there and had nannies and balls and crinolines. And there was one girl called Edith — "

26

"Stop, stop! Your mother's been making up stories for you again. You're a great pair, you two. Living in a dream world. What's this about an owl that screamed?"

"That really did happen, Max. It gave us an awful fright. It flew out of an attic window. I had a funny feeling for a minute that there was someone in the house. I'm like Kitty, I felt the place was haunted — "

Ella stopped as the telephone rang.

"Damn!" said Max. "Can't I be left in peace for an hour?"

"I'll get it, darling."

"If it's McIntosh tell him I'm not home yet. It it's Brady, I'll talk to him."

In the hall, sitting on the telephone seat, Ella answered briskly, and an unfamiliar voice said, "Is your husband home, Mrs. Simpson?"

Ella hesitated. That rather common voice was neither Brady's nor McIntosh's.

"Who is speaking, please?"

"That's none of your business, Mrs. Simpson. Just get your husband."

"Who is it, Ella?" Max called.

Ella held her hand over the receiver.

"I don't know. Someone who wants you.

He's rather impertinent.''

"Who the devil — " Max took the receiver from Ella, and said in his curtest business voice, "Simpson here.''

Then he listened, and Ella, a pace away, hearing the unintelligible mutter in the telephone, saw the tension lines come back to Max's mouth.

Bother! Some business problem, and Max scarcely home, and jaded from a hard trip. Well, let's hope Kitty doesn't mention her dear friend Sam again this evening, or any other controversial subject.

"I don't understand," Max was saying. "What are you getting at? . . . But I've just got home from a damned tiring trip. Why is it so important to see you tonight? . . . Who are you? . . . I said, who are you? . . . What? . . . What's that? . . . Who?''

As if he felt her anxious presence behind him, Max looked back at Ella, his expression disbelieving. Not at seeing her, of course, but at what he was hearing. He wasn't really seeing her at all, she realized. He was listening too intently.

The mysterious caller must have asked a question, for suddenly he replied in a sharp clipped voice, "Very well. In twenty minutes. And it had better be important."

He banged down the receiver, muttering, "Wasting my bloody time!" He only swore when he was tired, his temper frayed, his nerves stretched. Or when he encountered some overwhelming stupidity. His own brain was too sharp to tolerate easily other people's less-quick wits.

"What is it?" Ella asked.

"I have to go out."

"What for? Can't it wait?"

"No!"

"Don't you know what it's about?"

"I will shortly."

"But, Max — "

"For God's sake, Ella! It's bad enough having to go off on a wild-goose chase without you cross-examining me. It's important, this fellow says, so I'll have to take his word for it, won't I?"

"Don't you know who he is? But if he's someone from the office — "

Max was at the door. "I'll tell you when I get back."

Of course it must be someone from the office. Max wouldn't leave his half-finished supper, the half-empty bottle of wine, for anything else.

"That wretched office," Ella said. "Can't they leave you alone just when you get home?"

"It's what I'm paid for, love."

The door banged behind Max. In a few moments Ella heard his car start. So whoever he was meeting must be some distance away. Funny. He hadn't known who it was. He had been mystified before he became angry. He would hardly have let himself show anger to one of his confederates. But it must be something concerning the office. Some intrigue. Something to do with the export manager's position. Anything to do with that would receive top priority attention from Max.

Oh, well, she would know soon enough what this was all about. At least, as much as Max would tell her. He had always judged how much she should know. He thought women talked indiscreetly. He trusted her loyalty to him, but cautiousness was a deep instinct in him. Something to do with his insecure childhood. She did understand. She used infinite patience with him.

But it was a pity their supper was spoiled. Kitty was toying languidly with her bread and butter, her long hair hanging over her plate. A sure sign that she was upset when she hid behind a veil of hair. She was acutely sensitive. The ténsion she had heard in Max's voice would have communicated itself to her immediately. She hated loud voices, angry voices, worried voices. She was too gentle for this world, Ella thought.

"You've got to grow another skin, darling," she said absently.

"What sort of skin?" came Kitty's voice, muffled. "Like a lizard?"

"Any sort, just so long as you don't think the end of the world has come because Daddy has had to go out on business. He'll give you your present when he comes back. Anyway, it's tails lizards grow, not skins."

An hour later Max had not returned. The long dusk was turning into night although the heat remained, sticky and airless. Ella sat on one of the uncomfortable wrought-iron chairs on the small square of flagstones that Max called a patio, worrying a little, but not too much.

It was not Max going off so suddenly, but

the mood in which he had gone off, angry but uneasy, too. He might have thought he concealed his uneasiness, but she knew him too well. There must have been a crisis at the office since he had been away. Someone was warning him about it before he went in tomorrow.

He would be able to cope. He always did.

It was strange that she felt lonelier at this moment than when he was abroad. Kitty was in bed, there was nothing she wanted to watch on television, she had finished her library book, it was too hot to be indoors. And she was conscious of this vague nagging apprehension that had really been with her ever since she had thought someone watched her in that old empty house.

A light sprang on in the upstairs window of the Bramwell's house next door. She saw a man's head, looking exaggeratedly large because of thick shaggy dark hair, move near the window. He didn't look out, he wouldn't have been able to see her in the dark, anyway, but his presence gave her a certain amount of comfort. He was evidently having a night off from the theater. She could hear faintly dishes clattering in the kitchen where his sister must be doing the washing up.

The Bramwells, who had moved in recently, were pleasant but withdrawn neighbors, too intellectual for Max. What did you discuss with a theater critic or a librarian except the latest play or the latest book, neither of which he knew anything about. He was too busy with more constructive activities, such as boosting the country's exports.

But Ella sometimes nodded to Mr. Bramwell when he left his typewriter to stroll outdoors. She privately called him and his sister the Brontës. Literary and a little eccentric. She sometimes had the feeling that Mr. Bramwell watched her from his study window more than was apparent.

It didn't matter. Someone trying to create over a typewriter had to gaze out at something. If you came in his line of vision then you were watched.

The large dark head had disappeared again, and only a minute later the front door banged and Max was home.

Ella hurried indoors.

"Oh, darling, I'm so glad you're back. What was it?"

"What was what?"

He was prevaricating for some reason. So it was one of the things she was not to be told.

"This meeting. This man who wanted to see you so urgently."

"Ella, don't nag, please. I'm tired. I've had it for today."

Ella noticed his tense mouth, and an odd look of harassment in his eyes. Or was it shock? Had something serious happened?

"I wasn't nagging. I only wondered — Max, you look worried." She tried flippancy. "You haven't been found out cooking the company's books?"

His brows gathered.

"Don't be daft, Ella. At least, not more daft than — "

"Than usual?" she finished, deeply hurt.

An expression, half ashamed, flickered in his eyes and was gone.

"That's what I meant. As usual." He was making his voice joky, and good-humored, but the underlying accusation was there.

"You must admit you've been more than a bit absentminded lately."

"Have I? Why didn't you tell me?"

"I'm telling you now. It's only since your miscarriage. Quite understandable. I talked to the doctor about it."

Ella looked at him in surprise and some private distress.

"When? You didn't tell me."

"When I had my smallpox jab. Not to worry, love. He said it would pass."

Ella frowned. In some ways, and particularly where her husband was concerned, she was as sensitive as Kitty. How had this conversation about herself started?

"But what have I done? What specific thing? I mean, that I haven't been aware of."

Max was impatient again.

"Don't bother about it now. Let's go to bed. Rest was the important thing, the doctor said."

"Oh, he told me that, too. But only to get rid of my tiredness. Not for daftness."

Max kissed her briefly on the forehead.

"That's it, isn't it? Everyone's a bit daft

when they're tired. Look at all that fantasy about people in that old house you and Kitty found."

"Oh, you mean Edith and her family," Ella said, relieved. "I didn't know that had irritated you."

"Living in a dream world."

"No, that isn't true. There was once an Edith in that house. Her name is scratched on the windowpane."

But Max was off at a tangent.

"Since the doctor told you to rest, why do you go off on long walks with Kitty in weather like this? Don't do it again. That's an order. Now I'm going up to bed. Are you coming?"

"In a minute. When I've locked up. If you can trust me to do that."

Ella looked at his retreating back in hurt bewilderment. Whatever had happened tonight, why was he taking it out on her? Perhaps she was a bit forgetful, a bit dreamy. Losing the baby had been a much deeper grief to her than she had let him know. It would have been easier to bear had it been a shared grief, but she knew Max hadn't been too distressed. The baby had been a girl, and if they had another child he wanted it to be a boy. Otherwise, Kitty was enough. So she had ignored the doctor's warning about psychological shock and assumed a cheerful face. For Kitty's sake as well as Max's.

But had she exhibited symptoms of which she hadn't been aware?

That pretty innocent fantasy about Edith. Why should that have irritated Max so much unless, to him, it was evidence of more disturbing behavior? What nonsense! She was only a little imaginative and absentminded.

And Max was in a mood about the only thing that truly worried him, his position with the company. It wasn't fair but it was human nature, that he should take it out on someone, she, his wife, being the most effective person.

She went around the doors with her usual care, turning locks and fastening bolts. This was the kind of house that got burgled, detached and with a garden that backed onto fields. Not rich, but prosperous enough for the petty thief who was looking for radio sets or silver sports trophies or unspectacular jewelry. Max constantly emphasized that when he was away she must never neglect to lock up properly. When he was home he would do it, naturally.

But he hadn't tonight. Whatever was on his mind had made him forget. So she had to do it, going meticulously from windows to doors, and then turning off lights. One lived in an age of suspicion and apprehension. It didn't do to think too much about it.

When she went upstairs a little later Max was in bed and apparently asleep, although the bedside light was still on.

His worry couldn't be that bad, if it allowed him to fall asleep so quickly. She bent over him, loving his sleeping face, with its return to innocence. She thought she saw his eyelid flicker, and suddenly knew that he was pretending. Why, for goodness sake? Because he didn't want to make love to her? Could it be that? But didn't he guess that she might be relieved, on a hot night like this, to escape a sticky embrace?

As if he knew her thoughts, his eyes suddenly flew open, and she saw him look accusingly at the little alarm clock on the bedside table.

"Ella, for God's sake, it's half past twelve! Whatever took you so long?"

"No, it isn't, darling. I've only been ten minutes."

"Ten minutes! Two hours! Can't you tell the time?"

It was quite extraordinary, but the hands of the clock did point to half past twelve. She could have sworn it was only half past ten. At least, that had been the time when Max had come up. And she had only done the locking up since then.

"You've been in one of your dreams again," he said accusingly. "You just don't know time passes."

"But I haven't. I came straight up. Honestly!"

Max took her hand with unexpected gentleness and concern.

"You've forgotten. But don't worry, love. It's this memory thing. It will pass. Sorry if I bit your head off."

Tears of tiredness and bewilderment filled Ella's eyes. The clock did say half past twelve. Whatever was suddenly wrong with her?

"I haven't the faintest memory — "

"That's what I'm telling you. Amnesia's the word."

"But I've never had it before."

"Would you know? I've said not to worry. Come on, hurry up and get to bed. I'm practically dead. Got a splitting headache."

"Oh, darling. Shall I get you some aspirin?"

"No, just come to bed and put the light out."

What had happened to those two missing hours? What was happening to her so suddenly? Ella did sleep at last, only to dream about a tall man in somber black clothes, with a long curled black mustache, and holding a riding crop in an uplifted hand. Edith's father, she thought hazily, an old-fashioned villain who beat his wife and made her scream . . . so piercingly that her screams hung in the air for a hundred years afterward. . . .

Chapter 3

The sound of Max padding about the room
(he was not the quietest of risers) woke Ella.
Before she moved, she was conscious of a
drained tiredness which seemed entirely to
bear out what Max had said about her
health. It was the unaccustomed heat, of
course. Even at this early hour it was sultry
and oppressive.

"What's the time?" she asked.

"Half past seven," said Max, and flopped
down beside her.

"It's late! Why didn't you wake me?"

"You had a restless night. You were
talking in your sleep."

"I had a nightmare. I remember it now.
What did I say?"

"Something about don't touch me, and
then you gave little mews. Like a kitten.

Funny old thing."

"I dreamt that Victorian father had a riding crop. In that house."

"You see, love. It *was* all a dream."

She sat up. "Not yesterday. Oh, no, that was real. Because Kitty heard the scream, too."

"You told her she heard it, so she thinks she did." Max's voice sounded infinitely weary. He yawned heavily and closed his eyes.

Ella grew wider awake.

"You're not dressed. Aren't you in a hurry?"

"Not going to the office, love. I feel lousy. Must have caught a bug traveling. I'll stay home today. This morning, anyway. I might feel better later on."

"Oh, poor darling! You said you had a headache last night."

"I've still got it."

"I'll make you some tea. You could drink a nice cup of tea, couldn't you?"

Max lifted heavy eyelids and let them fall again. Ella assumed it was acquiescence.

"Will you ring the office, or shall I?"

"I will. Later. They can't complain. I

haven't had a day off in five years."

"I know. They certainly can't complain. What about what happened last night?"

"What happened?"

"I'm asking you. Your meeting with your colleague."

"Your colleague!" Max mimicked. "Dear precise Ella."

"Well, I don't know who it was, do I?"

"No. You've never met him, love. He's in a spot of bother, and wants me to put in a word for him."

So that was all it had been last night. Ella felt relief. It must have been this illness coming on, not someone else's trouble, that had put that look of shock in Max's eyes.

"What's the man done?" she asked.

"I can't tell you that. You're too honest, love."

"What do you mean?"

"You prattle, like all ingenuous people. I wouldn't change you. At least, not much."

His grin didn't quite succeed in being lighthearted.

"Then is it something dishonest this man has done?"

"There you are, you see. You're

43

disapproving already. You'd want to go and report him, where I might want to give him another chance. That's the difference between us."

Ella frowned. "I do dislike dishonesty."

"That's what I'm saying. So if you don't know about this, you won't be worried. Remember that time you got my driving license endorsed?"

"But that accident was your fault, Max. It wasn't fair not to say so."

"Okay, okay. That's what I mean. Your compulsive honesty. You nearly broke up our marriage that time."

Ella nodded slowly, remembering that painful experience. After a pause she said carefully, "So are you going to help this man — whatever he's done?"

"I haven't made up my mind. For God's sake, don't cross-examine me now, Ella. I can't think."

"No, darling. Of course you can't." Ella put her hand on his forehead. It felt hot, but her hand was hot, too. Everything was hot on this airless morning. "I'll go and make that tea."

"And keep Kitty quiet, if you can," Max

called after her. "And bring up the morning paper."

"Darling, if your head's so bad — "

"I only want to read the headlines, for Pete's sake."

After she had left him with the papers, she heard his gasp. She went back into the room quickly, thinking him ill.

He was sitting up in bed, that flat look of shock back in his face.

"What is it, Max?"

He gave her an exasperated look as if she were intruding unwarrantably on his suffering.

"Fabritex shares have dropped ten pence. That's all I needed."

"If that's all," said Ella in relief, "I'll bring up your tea."

She hurried downstairs, calling to Kitty on the way. "Hurry up, darling, it's nearly eight o'clock."

It was only when Max had drunk two cups of tea, but eaten nothing, and Kitty was halfway through her cereal, that Ella thought of something odd. Max had not had the paper open at the stock market page when he had made that announcement about the shares dropping in value. It had been spread out uncreased and apparently unopened on the coverlet. Surely Fabritex shares didn't warrant a front-page announcement? She would look later.

If her memory was as bad as Max said it was, of course, she would forget all about it. And that might be a good thing. Why worry over something about which she could do nothing?

"Ella!" Max was calling downstairs again.

"Yes, darling?"

"Are you taking Kitty to school?"

"Of course I am. You know I always do."

"Do you drop her at the gate? And see that she goes right in?"

"Usually. Unless she sees her boyfriend Sam coming and wants to wait for him."

"Well, don't let her. Don't have her hanging about on the street. Watch her until she's inside the door."

"Aren't you being a bit fussy, all at once? It's a very quiet street. Anyway, Kitty's sensible. She wouldn't run out into traffic."

"She's just about as dreamy as her mother."

"What does that mean?" Ella asked.

"It means she's liable to do unpredictable things. Apart from that, you know what can happen to kids nowadays. Blond little girls, in particular."

Ella did know. It was an ever-present anxiety. Kitty with her big trusting blue eyes, and floating hair, was natural prey. It was one of the biggest indictments against modern society that the innocence of children had to be destroyed by warnings about evil in the world.

She wondered vaguely why Max was worrying about this particular problem just now, then realized that usually he had left for the office by the time she took Kitty to school. Also, his frail condition this morning was making him overanxious.

"I'll be careful," she called. "Try to have a sleep while we're gone. Is there anything you want me to get for you?"

"Yes, you might try to remember my shaving cream. I've asked you three times to get it. Do you have secret hankerings to have a husband with a beard?"

"You haven't asked me for it at all!" Ella protested. "I'm sure I'd remember."

His voice came down the stairs, infinitely weary. "That's what I've been trying to tell you, love. You're forgetting everything these days. Absolutely everything."

Ella knitted her brows, not listening to Kitty's chatter, as she drove down the long tree-lined street in the direction of the school. *Had* Max asked her to get him shaving cream? She was sure he had a half-full tube in the bathroom, anyway. Another thing she must check when she returned. If she remembered, she thought ironically. She really would be as vague as Max insisted she was if he kept on throwing these accusations at her.

"Mummy, can I tell Sam about our house, and Edith and her crinoline?" Kitty said happily.

"Do you think little boys are interested in that sort of thing, darling?"

"He'd be interested in the owl and the scream," Kitty said with certainty.

"Daddy says we didn't really hear a scream. He says we imagined it because we were making up stories. I expect he's right."

"But we *saw* the owl."

"Yes, we did, didn't we? Anyway, forget about it now. It's all a bit eerie for little girls."

"Eerie," said Kitty, testing another new word. "Eerie, eerie, eerie."

Ella watched her safely into the school grounds, as Max had insisted she do, then decided against doing any shopping. She was anxious to get home to Max. She hoped he wasn't really ill. She was still convinced that his sudden accusations about her tiredness and vagueness were a symptom of his own state of health. Had he pushed himself too hard, and was starting a breakdown?

All the same, that unexplained problem of missing two hours last night was extremely puzzling. Could she have sat down and fallen asleep without remembering doing so?

She drove home a little too fast, turning into the drive with a screech of brakes, then pulling up sharply as she found the parking space already occupied by a police car!

Panic exploded in her head. Kitty? No, Kitty was safely at school. Max? Safely in bed. She tumbled out of the car and ran into the house, to find Max in his dressing gown calmly entertaining two policemen in the lounge.

"She won't be long," Ella heard him saying. "Oh, here she is now. Ella, come in here. These gentlemen want to ask you a question."

"Me!" Ella gasped, already guilty. "What is it? Have I been speeding?"

"I hope not," said Max. He came to put an arm around her protectively. "Though I was explaining that you haven't been well. I'm not sure how reliable your evidence will be."

"Evidence!"

"We're just making routine inquiries about a stolen car, ma'am," one of the constables said, with a precise pleasing courtesy. "Did you by any chance notice a four-liter 1966 gray Jaguar in this vicinity at any time yesterday afternoon?"

"Parked?" Ella asked foolishly.

"More likely speeding. Going fast enough for you to notice."

"No, I didn't. So many cars go past. Besides, I was out most of the afternoon."

"Keep to the point, darling," Max said. "The constable only wants to know about the car. I've told him about your bad memory. She's not a very observant person, constable. In a dream, mostly, aren't you, love?"

Ella frowned, a memory eluding her. It was perfectly true that she was forgetful. But did Max have to keep on insisting on it to a couple of policemen? As if he had an idiot wife.

"I'm sorry I can't help you," she said. "Are you asking at every house in the street?"

"Yes, ma'am."

"What's happened? A bank robbery?"

"It could be worse than that, ma'am. If anything comes to your mind, would you give us a ring at this number?"

The constable with the notebook handed her a card with a telephone number on it. "Just anything at all that you think significant."

Significant. That was a word Kitty would find interesting. Significant, meaning sinister. . . .

"Worse than a bank robbery," she murmured.

"If my wife can't help you — " Max hinted.

The policemen moved to the door.

"Thank you, sir. Thank you, ma'am. We hope we won't have to trouble you again."

Ella giggled a little as they went. "Wasn't that rather sweet and old-fashioned, Max, calling me ma'am? I was going to tell them about that empty house, but you stopped me."

"I know. You were only wasting their time. They wanted to know about a stolen car, not a derelict house. Anyway, I think you and Kitty dreamed up that house and family."

"The family, perhaps. Not the house. If you don't believe me I'll take you there."

"For God's sake, I'm bored with it," Max said, with sudden explosive tension. "The police have a crime on their hands and you natter on about an old house."

"What is the crime?" Ella asked, struck with a queer apprehension.

"No crime at all, in my opinion. A stupid

52

woman has disappeared. Run off with her lover, obviously."

"In a gray Jaguar?"

"Who knows? Her family think she's been kidnapped, and a Jaguar has been reported stolen. The two things probably have no connection."

Ella's mind had taken in only one word. She had known there was something sinister.

"Kidnapped!" She was testing the word, like Kitty.

"Who'd be crazy enough to kidnap a grown woman?" Max said. "I'm surprised at the police taking it seriously."

"There must be some reason for them doing that, some evidence."

"And since you haven't got a legal mind, love, just forget it. Just use your little scatterbrain for remembering the important things. Like not being late for picking Kitty up this afternoon, and having my dinner ready when I get home."

"Where did this woman live?"

"Miles from here. In one of those big houses near Ascot. She's just another rich bitch with a lover."

"Children?"

"I believe so. I told you to forget it. Make me some coffee, will you, darling? I'm going to get dressed and go to the office."

"Are you feeling better?"

He nodded. "I had a migraine, I think. It's going off."

"I'm so glad. I'll put the coffee on right away."

"Bless you." Max kissed her forehead. "And don't forget to turn the element off afterward."

"Of course I won't. Why are you getting so suspicious of me?"

"Because you left it on earlier. I found it after you'd taken Kitty to school. We haven't all that money to waste on electricity."

"I *can't* have!"

"Your word against mine, love. There it was, red hot."

Ella felt tears of exasperation and bewilderment come into her eyes. Who was imagining things, she or Max? It was he who had had a migraine (she never remembered him having one before) but was now better, as if the police visit had

54

stimulated and revived him.

"You won't be nervous, will you?" Max called from upstairs.

"About being alone? Good heavens, no. I'm not a rich bitch to be kidnapped."

Although she was suddenly remembering what had eluded her when the police had been there, the faint haze, as of dust stirred by a car, after the owl had flown from the window of the empty house. Had it been stirred by a gray Jaguar? Now she was doing what Max said was so dangerous, mixing fantasy with reality.

Max was coming downstairs, tucking his shirt in.

"Don't go for lonely walks, that's all. You might forget to pick up Kitty."

"Max, don't be so *absurd*. Why are you harping on Kitty? You know I never forget to pick up her up."

"But are you always punctual?"

"Of course I am. More or less."

"Then make it more. Kitty's a nice-looking kid. I don't need to tell you that." He came to her and rumpled her hair. "Don't look so worried. And have a rest after I've gone. You really do look tired.

Look at these shadows under your eyes."

Ella jerked away. "Oh, leave me alone, stop fussing." She was finding his sudden solicitousness intensely irritating, and strangely unnerving. "What are you going to do about that man?"

"Man?"

She was certain that flash in his eyes, gone immediately, was alarm.

"The one at the office in trouble. You can't have forgotten. The one who rang you last night."

"Oh, him. Oh, I've sorted that out. I'll take his side."

"I'm glad."

"Glad?"

"I like you to be kind. I sometimes think business doesn't allow much kindness."

"Nor sentiment. Strictly out. Except for a little in my wife." He gave her a gentle slap. "Hurry up with that coffee. And ring me if you're worried."

"What should I be worried about?"

"Well, if the police come back, or anything."

"They're not likely to, are they?"

"I shouldn't think so. I don't think I'd

mention that fantasy about an empty house, if they do."

"Why ever not?"

"Because they might think you're a bit loony, love. They get plenty of loony witnesses. Those big eyes of yours. Just like Kitty's, but she's entitled to believe in fairy stories, at her age. A Victorian husband with a horsewhip. Oh, dear, oh, dear!"

"I only *dreamt* that," Ella protested.

But had she? Hadn't it been strongly in her mind yesterday, when the scream had rung out? As if she had seen vividly into the past, and known that Edith's father (or husband, for Edith might have been the wife) had had moments of sadistic cruelty.

As perhaps all men had.

Was she really being a bit daft, or was Max's insistence on it his latent form of cruelty? A more subtle way of achieving power over his wife than the Victorians had exercised.

Now you are daft, Ella, she told herself, as she allowed Max to give her a particularly loving good-bye kiss. He cared about her state of health.

Or, by his unaccustomed gentleness, was

he deliberately impressing on her her fragility?

She sat down at the kitchen table and cried a little when he had gone. She was so bewildered.

Chapter 4

Mrs. Ingram arrived, as usual, at ten o'clock. She hung up her plastic raincoat (without which she never stirred outdoors, she was one of those perennially suspicious of the weather), put on an apron, her old flip-flop slippers which she kept in the broom cupboard, and, spry and perky on her broomstick legs, was ready for work.

At least she would be ready when she had oiled the wheels, as she expressed it, with a cup of the coffee she knew Ella would have kept hot for her. She prided herself on being a coffee drinker. She thought tea was common, suitable only for charwomen, of which race she was decidedly not a member. She was a professional domestic help, though Ella was ignorant of the finer points of that definition.

A cup of milky coffee sweetened with three spoons of sugar, and the morning's quota of gossip.

"Well, now, Mrs. Simpson, that poor woman."

"What poor woman?" Ella asked, pretending ignorance of such a distasteful and disturbing subject. She was still in a state of tension following the visit of the two policemen.

"As is kidnapped. She'll never be found alive!"

"You don't want to believe everything you read in the papers, Mrs. Ingram."

"This ain't only in the papers. It was on the telly, too. They showed her picture. A nice-looking lady. Young and pretty, dressed for a ball or something. She had some earrings those kidnappers would get their hands on. Real sparklers."

"My husband says it's much more likely she's run off with a lover."

"Then why was there signs of a struggle?" Mrs. Ingram's small polished black eyes were always bright with some indignation. "Why is the police making inquiries? They was here, I heard."

"But not about a missing woman, only a missing car. They went to every house in the street."

"The kidnap vehicle," Mrs. Ingram said knowledgeably.

Was it? Ella hadn't thought of that. She said too vehemently, "Mrs. Ingram, you watch too much television. You begin to think crime. That's why I'm so careful about what I let Kitty see."

"I'm not a child in arms, Mrs. Simpson."

"No, but you're a bit brainwashed. Like most of us," Ella added quickly, anxious to avoid Mrs. Ingram's sulphurous indignation. "Anyway, this will never get a morning's work done. I'll do the beds if you'll get on with the downstairs."

Mrs. Ingram gave her glittering stare a moment longer, then flip-flopped resignedly to the sink, and the breakfast dishes. Although she was by no means finished with the subject.

"What'd you tell the police, Mrs. Simpson?"

"Why, that I hadn't seen the gray Jaguar, of course."

"A Jag, was it? Aye, that's the kind that

gets used for these jobs. It's speed they want. Poor lady. They'd have her from here to Brighton before she knew what had hit her."

"Was she hit?" Ella asked involuntarily.

"The hall furniture was knocked over, wasn't it? The telephone was on the floor, and a bowl of roses spilt all over the place. She musta bin hit, with that struggling going on. Tied up, I dessay."

"It could have been arranged, couldn't it, to mislead people?"

"Why? If she just wanted to walk out, she could walk out, couldn't she? Without breaking up the furniture. That's what it said in the paper. Didn't you read it?"

"Not everyone has time to read the morning paper in the morning."

"Lor bless you!" Mrs. Ingram's voice had taken on its benevolent quality, used whenever she thought Ella a lovable but idiot child. "Listening to you, anyone wouldn't believe there was wickedness in the world. But there is. You'll find out, more's the pity."

"I'm not ignorant." Ella's voice was testy. "I know terrible things happen. I just don't believe they will ever happen to us, to Kitty or Max or me. If that's being ignorant, then I'm glad I am. You couldn't go about expecting disaster all the time, or you'd go dotty." Ella winced privately at the word she had used, but added determinedly, "Mrs. Ingram, have you noticed me being absentminded lately? I mean, forgetting things."

Mrs. Ingram's thin body bent with her dry breathless laughter. She was a dried seedpod shaking in the wind.

"Lor, yes, Mrs. Simpson, you're the dreamiest lady I ever worked for. Half the time you don't even hear what I say. But it don't upset me. It's just your way."

"No, more serious things than that, Mrs. Ingram. For example, like accidentally setting fire to the house."

"You ain't done that yet. But I wouldn't trust you with matches, that I wouldn't."

Was Mrs. Ingram joking, in her slightly macabre way? Or not?

Ella found she didn't care to ask.

"I know I'm dreamy. I know I've been worse since the baby."

"Natural," said Mrs. Ingram.

"I have to pull myself together. Last night I lost a whole two hours. Just lost them." She saw Mrs. Ingram's incomprehension and laughed. "I only must have fallen asleep. It was so hot, wasn't it? It's going to be hot again today. I'll fill the play pool so Kitty can cool herself off when she comes home. I expect she'll have Sam with her. Is she young enough for mixed bathing in the nude?"

"Innocent little darling," said Mrs. Ingram. The expression in her eyes, worldly and sharply knowing, said that Kitty's mother wasn't much less innocent.

"I did want that baby," Ella murmured. "More than anyone knows."

"That was a real shame, Mrs. Simpson, but you gotta realize England's stuffed full of people. Won't be room to lie down soon, they say. We'll all have to die standing up." Mrs. Ingram gave her creaky laughter again, then, studying Ella, had a moment of rare sentiment. "Though a nicer lady couldn't bring kids into the world. Take that kidnapped madam, now. I'll bet she only had hers by accident. Now they're at one of them posh boarding schools. You see, she don't really want to be bothered with them. Thinking of her horse racing and her parties. They say the kidnappers either wanted money or they got a grudge against her husband. Or both, I dessay. You got shopping to do? What are you having for dinner tonight?"

Dinner seemed so far off. There was the long hot day to be lived through before Max was home. Mrs. Ingram's busy tongue was going to be more trying than usual, but Ella was already half-dreading lunchtime when Mrs. Ingram would put on her plastic mac and depart, and the house would be empty.

She must be getting neurotic. She had never been afraid of an empty house, she usually enjoyed it.

There was plenty to do, Max's bags to be unpacked and his laundry sorted, the beds to make, the shopping list to prepare.

But already Ella was idling upstairs, sitting on the unmade bed reading the paper which Max had left flung on the floor.

She couldn't find the stock market page, and only realized after a five-minute search that prices were not listed on Mondays. Max must have read about the Fabritex shares in a small item somewhere else.

The kidnapping had headlines. There was a picture of a large house, with its terrace and swimming pool, from which the woman was alleged to have been taken, and an inset photograph of her. A pretty smiling coquettish face, and the long expensive earrings Mrs. Ingram had mentioned. Her name was Daphne Gibson. Her husband, Bernard Gibson, was president of a construction company, and a millionaire. There were two daughters, aged eight and ten, at boarding school.

The house hadn't been ransacked. Nothing (except Mrs. Gibson) appeared to be missing. And there was the disarray in the hall where the struggle had taken place. It was thought that either Mrs. Gibson had recognized her callers (it was assumed that there were two), or else she had been rather careless in allowing strange men inside the front door.

She had been alone in the house at the time. It was her butler's day off and her housekeeper, her only other living-in servant, appeared to have been absent also. The housekeeper had eventually returned, indignant and alarmed, saying that she had got a telephone message to say that her elderly mother was ill, but when she arrived at her home in a neighboring village it was only to find her mother hale and hearty weeding the garden.

The kidnap note had been propped up on the mantelpiece in the best tradition of a fleeing wife, but its contents had been far from the apology of an unfaithful wife. It had said simply, "We got your wife. Wait instructions. Keep away from police."

The police, it seemed, shared Max's view, and thought the whole thing a hoax. But routine inquiries were being made. No doubt Mr. Bernard Gibson was a man who could kick up a stink if he thought insufficient attention was being given to the safe recovery of his wife. He had certainly not been intimidated by the kidnappers' instructions, for he must have instantly called in the police.

But who would have the audacity or the sheer stupidity to kidnap a grown woman? Unless it was never intended that she should return home. . . .

Ella kept thinking of the gray Jaguar

speeding down the road, actually past this house, with the terrified prisoner in the back. It must have happened while she and Kitty were on their long walk. She was always disgusted with the cowardly people who refused to give evidence because they didn't want to be involved, but in this case she was deeply thankful that she had nothing to tell. It would be terrifying, she sensed. Kidnappers were desperate people. It was such a cold-blooded crime. One didn't want even to think of it.

Anyway, it was probably, as Max said, nothing but a hoax. Mrs. Daphne Gibson looked as if she would have a taste for the theatrical. Perhaps she was punishing her husband for something.

Now what was it Max had told her to be careful about today? Oh, yes, not being late for Kitty. He had been thinking of Mrs. Gibson's kidnapping, she supposed. But Kitty was only a little girl and hadn't even got rich parents. She wasn't the kind of prey for kidnappers — if there were actually such people. Max was in a nervous state, what with coming home tired, and having to go out on that mysterious errand, then developing a violent headache. He had been exaggerating domestic problems, such as her own vagueness, simply to compensate for his more real business ones. She hoped everything was going well at the office today, otherwise he would come home overtired and irritable.

The struggle for the throne (as she privately called it) was getting too important and too nerve-wracking. Export manager. It really sounded rather prosaic. She simply couldn't see it in the vivid and irresistible colors that Max could.

At midday the telephone rang, and it was Max, which was another unlikely thing. He seldom called her from the office.

"Hullo, darling, everything all right?"

"Of course it is. Why shouldn't it be?"

"Why, indeed?" His voice sounded falsely hearty. "Mrs. Ingram there?"

"Yes."

"Good. She'll keep an eye on you."

Ella was annoyed. This was getting beyond a joke.

"Is that all you rang me for, to see if Mrs. Ingram was keeping an eye on me?"

"No, no, don't get on your high horse.

I've had a bit of good news. I'm getting the new car a month earlier than I expected. Isn't that something in this day and age? It should arrive tomorrow. So you'll have to stay in to take delivery."

The new car was a Rover. Max had set his heart on it, but had only been able to order it after she had had her miscarriage. If the baby had been born they wouldn't have been able to afford a new car for another year.

Max had thought it would cheer her up, and even compensate her for the loss of the baby. This was one of the occasions when their minds functioned at opposite poles.

She was going to hate that new car passionately. Even if she told him why, she was afraid Max wouldn't understand. It was simply that she was a woman and deeply sentimental, he was a man, and coolly, admirably practical.

"Oh, and by the way, Max, those shares. I couldn't find where they'd dropped."

"What shares?"

"Fabritex, of course. You told me this morning."

"My dear girl, what *are* you talking

70

about? I never mentioned any shares. How could I? There aren't any stock market quotations on a Monday."

"But you said — I mean, you were upset, you got a headache because of it."

"Because of shares dropping! But they haven't. I've today's quotations right in front of me."

"Then why did you look so shocked this morning?"

"Me shocked! It was you who was, after that dream of your husband beating you."

"Not *my* husband." This conversation was ridiculous. They were utterly at cross-purposes.

"Well, he will if you take up any more of his time talking nonsense."

"You did have a headache. You were worried," she said defensively.

"So I was about O'Brien's foolishness. But that problem has sorted itself out, thank goodness. I was worried about you, too, the odd way you were behaving. How do you feel now?"

"I feel fine, thank you," Ella said stiffly.

"Not overdoing it?"

"For heaven's sake, Max, there's nothing

the matter with me, and I can't stand this fussing. I simply don't understand why you're doing it."

"That's the trouble," Max said ominously. "Your funny little head is in a boggle. This talk of Fabritex shares, for instance. When have I ever discussed shares with you?"

That was true. He never did. It was this that had made the whole thing so surprising.

"But not to worry," his voice came, suddenly soothing. "I'll be home early this evening, I promise. If it's still hot we might take Kitty and go to the club for a swim. It's the heat that's affecting you. Me, too, with that headache. I don't get headaches normally. We're simply not used to this sort of weather."

She had scarcely hung up, rubbing her damp hands together agitatedly, before the telephone rang again.

This time, rather disturbingly, it was the strange voice of the previous evening. At least Ella was almost certain it was. It had a similar flippant common quality.

"Is that Mr. Max Simpson's residence?"

"Yes, it is, but my husband is at the

office, as you ought to know. Wasn't it you who rang last night?"

"Am I speaking to Mrs. Simpson?"

"I'm Mrs. Simpson," Ella answered cautiously.

"The very lady I want. Just a word of advice, love. Drive carefully."

The receiver clicked. The strange common voice, as if it had floated in through the ether, had gone.

And Ella was suddenly shaking, overcome by the feeling that she had been trying to hold at bay all morning. She could name it now. A feeling of menace. And evil.

She clasped her hands tightly together, making them stop trembling. Only when she had succeeded in this was she able to dial the office and ask for Max.

He was there quickly, as if, when he was told his wife wanted him, so soon after just speaking to him, he was not surprised. As if he had been expecting something like this. Or some other bizarre behavior from her.

"Max, I've just had the oddest telephone call."

"What was it?" She was relieved that his

voice wasn't impatient, simply crisp and questioning, though with an underlying urgency.

"A man with a very common voice has just told me to be careful driving."

"Really?" There was a pause. "What did you say?"

"He didn't give me time to say anything. He hung up."

"Something to do with the new car delivery, I expect."

"But he didn't mention the car. He seemed to be warning me. He sounded serious. Sinister."

"Then if it isn't someone from the garage it must be a joke. One of these telephone perverts. They get kicks out of frightening women. You're not scared, are you?"

"I am, a little. That kidnapping has got on my mind."

"But that's nothing remotely to do with you. It's miles away. Anyway it's only the usual newspaper sensationalism. Forget it. And don't worry about the telephone. It can't bite you."

Suddenly he, too, had become flippant. As if now he knew nothing serious was wrong, the problem was trivial and annoyingly time-consuming. But at first he had been apprehensive. Expectant. He couldn't deceive her. She knew every inflection of his voice. She might not be clever, but she was abnormally sensitive about other people, her husband in particular.

"You're not taking this seriously," she accused.

"Frankly, I'm not, darling. Unreliable little monsters, telephones. They play tricks on gullible women."

"Gullible?"

"Fanciful, love. Look, I'm up to my eyes. I'm due at a meeting in two minutes. Get Mrs. Ingram to answer the telephone if you're nervous. Have a rest this afternoon. But don't fall asleep and be late for Kitty."

Drive carefully. Don't be late for Kitty. The two admonitions might have been made by the same person, except that the voices were different.

No one trusted her today. Not even an anonymous telephone caller.

She went downstairs to find that Partridge, the gardener, had arrived. Mrs.

Ingram was out on the terrace talking to him. They both simultaneously turned their heads to look in the lounge window. When they saw her looking out they rather hastily separated, Mrs. Ingram bustling back to the kitchen, Partridge reaching a leisurely hand for the clippers. He was under Max's thumb, Partridge. Ella was sure he reported every flower she picked.

But he was kind to Kitty. Once he had made her a doll by tying twigs together and Kitty had been enchanted with it until it disintegrated. Ella was afraid he thought her the slightly scatty social type on account of her long pale hair and her cultivated voice. He talked to her much as he did to Kitty, with amused tolerance. When once she had said she would love to have a clump of spiky blue-green thistles in one of the corners of the garden he had said, "Them weeds. Mr. Simpson wouldn't care for them," and the subject was closed.

It wasn't her garden any more than it was her house, because she had been unable (or hadn't wanted?) to make her own mark on them. Partridge thought her a pleasant, amenable weak creature. Nothing to be

76

surprised about if she was suddenly getting fancies and doing odd things.

So she couldn't talk to him about the telephone call. Actually, now Max had dismissed it as unimportant, there was no one she could talk to.

She should have made friends in this district, the parents of other schoolchildren, for instance. But Max had discouraged it. He hadn't time to get involved in dull suburban parties. They were not here forever. They would soon be moving to a district where it would pay to cultivate the neighbors. Collingham was only transitional, a convenient stop on a train journey. They had had to stay here longer than he had expected, but it wouldn't be long now. He had promised to give her carte blanche with the new house.

When she went to collect Kitty at four o'clock, she did what the strange voice had exhorted, she drove with special care. Indeed, she was so cautious at the crossing over the busy High Street that the car behind her hooted impatiently. She couldn't see its driver's face in her mirror clearly because he wore a pulled-down hat. It seemed to be sharp and narrow and bad-tempered. She would never have been able to identify it again, she thought idly, then wondered why such a thought had occurred to her. Her mind was running on criminals today.

This impatient driver was completely anonymous, though he did shoot past her dangerously close when the lights changed. He almost scraped the side of the car. That would have made Max really furious, since he was trading it in tomorrow. But all was well. The other man was just a reckless driver. He couldn't have been deliberately giving her a fright, he couldn't have been the warning voice on the telephone.

That sort of thinking was just too bizarre.

Kitty wanted to bring Sam home. She said he was allowed to come.

Ella looked at the pugnacious, freckled six-year-old face of Sam, and wondered again at Kitty's choice of friends.

"Did your mother give your permission?" she asked.

"Yes, Mrs. Simpson. She said I could come until six o'clock."

Ella sighed. "Very well. Get in."

"I've told Sam about the house, Mummy," Kitty said. "He wants to go."

"Good gracious, no."

"But, Mummy — "

"It's much too far, and it's much too late. You'd never get back by dark. Besides, you couldn't go alone."

"Sam's got his gun."

"I'd shoot that old owl, Mrs. Simpson," said Sam, flourishing a very businesslike gun.

"Then the children could come out in the garden and play," said Kitty.

"What children?" Ella's eyes were on the driving mirror. She was still nervous about that dangerous driver.

"Oh, Mummy, the ones you told me about. You can't have forgotten."

Forgotten. That was a word that was being used much too frequently.

"No, darling, but they're only made-up children. I don't think Sam would care for them. You play mothers and fathers in your own garden with your own children."

"Dolls!" said Sam contemptuously.

Kitty bounced on the back seat, her innocent face tilted toward Sam beguilingly.

"They're not dolls, they're children, and you're their father. You have to promise not to beat them and make them scream like Edith's father did."

"Kitty!" said Ella sharply.

"We heard Edith yesterday. We really did, Sam. We had to run away from that garden. That's why I said to bring your gun."

"Kitty, you make up too many stories!"

Ella, you're imagining things again. . . .

'I'll beat all the children," said Sam. "Like this." He pounded happily at the car seat, and Kitty went into peals of adoring laughter. Whatever did she see in this tough little boy? Was she going to have a penchant for sadistic men?

"This is a very silly conversation," Ella said. "Anyway, it's too hot for exhausting games. I've filled the pool. You can play in that."

Sam certainly wasn't the best influence on Kitty. He got her overexcited and she became as noisy as he. Splashing in the pool, the dolls' pram with its multitudinous inhabitants parked safely out of harm's way, their voices grew so penetrating that the upstairs window of the house next door opened and Mr. Bramwell's shaggy dark head hung out.

"I say, Mrs. Simpson, on the principle that if you can't beat 'em, you join 'em, can I come over?"

Ella sprang up from her chair on the patio.

"I'm so sorry. Are the children making too much noise?"

"It's only that you can't keep windows shut in this weather. Glorious, isn't it? Mustn't complain."

"Will you come down and have some iced tea? Or beer?"

"May I? Having invited myself — "

Ella looked up at the indistinct face. She would like to see it closer. It was time she got to know her neighbors, anyway.

"It's no trouble at all. I was going to make some cool drinks. I'm afraid trying to keep the children quiet would be a losing battle."

"Be with you."

Presently he clambered over the back fence. He was broad-shouldered and heavily built, but obviously not the athletic type.

"I've seen you out of my study window."

"I know."

"Hope you didn't think I was a Peeping Tom."

"Goodness, no."

"I have my desk there. I find I look more at distant horizons than the work in my typewriter."

"Well I've heard it said that writers are working even when they're looking out of the window."

"Writers, Mrs. Simpson, are full of the biggest humbug of any profession. Anyway, I'm a critic, a species generally despised by legitimate writers."

He had a disproportionately high forehead, heavy black brows, and brilliant, rather sad black eyes. His appearance was a little formidable, even dressed as he was in a crumpled cotton shirt and baggy trousers. What had she to say to an egghead like this? Max would inquire amusedly.

What had she indeed? She only knew that it was nice to have company on this long hot uneasy afternoon.

She poured lemonade for the children and iced tea in glasses decorated with mint leaves for themselves.

"Yours?" inquired her visitor, as Kitty and Sam hurtled over.

"Only Kitty. She has an overdeveloped mother complex, and Sam, for some reason, seems to fulfill her idea of a father for her dozen or so children."

"She's never heard of the pill?"

"Goodness, no. That's not in Kitty's world. I'm afraid she's been born a century too late. We discovered a derelict Victorian house yesterday, and we literally saw all the children who had once lived there. Or Kitty did."

"You, too, I fancy?"

She nodded. "Kitty and I have extraordinarily similar reactions. I don't know whether that's a good thing or not." She looked into his observant black eyes and heard herself saying, "I lost a baby three months ago. I had so much wanted another child. Max — my husband — didn't mind so much. It would have been a girl and he wanted a boy."

"Another girl like Kitty. That's a tragedy, Mrs. Simpson."

A feeling of deep gratitude filled her.

"Don't call me Mrs. Simpson. I'm Ella. That was a nice thing you just said."

"I'm all for blue-eyed Kittys in this world. Where was the old house?"

"Across the fields. About two miles away, I should think. There's an overgrown garden. Max says it must be a place scheduled for demolition. It looks as if it's been empty for years, except for owls. Oh, by the way, did the police call on you this morning about that car?"

"They did."

"Had you seen it?"

"No. Anyway, I never pay any attention to cars going by. Who does?"

"Do you think that woman has been kidnapped? Max says it's a hoax."

"Probably it is. I can't see anyone in his right mind taking an adult person — but criminals aren't supposed to be in their right minds, are they? Can I have some more of this delicious tea?"

Ella picked up the jug.

"I've been thinking too much about it. Especially since the police came. It's made us seem a part of it, and yet what can we do?"

"Nothing."

"She isn't a very appealing woman from her photograph. Max says she's a playgirl. But I still keep thinking — " Ella shrugged apologetically. "Kitty and I got caught up in that story I made up about the old house, and the people in it. Then an owl flew out of an upstairs window with a screech and it was like a nightmare. I couldn't seem to shake it off, somehow. I got awfully absentminded. Max got quite worried. It was the heat, too. Nothing seemed quite real. It still doesn't."

"Not even me?"

"I confess I've been calling you Mr. Brontë to myself. What's your first name?"

"Booth."

Again she was embarrassed, second thoughts coming too slowly.

"I should have known it, shouldn't I?"

"Only if you read the papers I write for, the *Chronicle* and the *Aspect.*"

"They're a little highbrow — I mean, Max prefers more financial papers. Money papers, I call them. He isn't one for the arts. He hasn't time."

"And you?"

Ella shrugged again. "Living out here, it's such a trek to the West End. And I never cared about leaving Kitty."

"My sister would look after her. She works in the London Library. When she gets home she never wants to go out again."

"What a kind thought. I'll mention it to Max."

"I'll tell you when there's something worth seeing. I mean, in my presumptuous view."

"Thank you," said Ella, with her spontaneous air of delight. "My husband isn't really a theatergoer, but I am. At least, given the opportunity. Max is entirely practical, and I'm the opposite. He says we keep each other's wilder aberrations in check."

"Do you have wild aberrations?"

"Oh, I do. I don't suppose you could say Max does much, unless you could call his passion for a neat garden with the biggest and best flowers an aberration. And his ambition. But a man should be ambitious."

"In what way?"

"To get to the top of his profession, of course. Don't you want to do that?" Ella put her hand to her mouth. "Now I've said the wrong thing again. I expect you are at the top."

"Such as it is." He smiled. He had a nice slow smile. "And if I want to stay there, I'd better get back to my typewriter. Thank you for the interlude. Do call out if you want anything. I'm usually in my study. Or Lorna's home when I'm gone."

What should she want? She had managed for quite a long time without a Booth Bramwell next door. She admitted to herself, however, that the thought of his solid presence behind the upstairs window was quite reassuring. And if that wasn't a very sensible word to use, it was the only one that occurred to her.

Chapter 5

Max threw the evening paper down as he came in. Ella, lifting her face for his kiss, was trying to read the headlines.

KIDNAP MYSTERY.... "Is there any news of that poor woman?" she asked.

"Only bogus telephone calls. Whew! I'm all in. The temperature was ninety in the city. I hope you've put some beer in the fridge."

"What do you mean by bogus telephone calls?"

Max looked at her sharply.

"You haven't had another, have you?"

"No, I haven't. But mine was nothing to do with the kidnapping, was it?"

Max went into the kitchen to open the refrigerator and take out one of the cool misted bottles. He took his time in answering.

"The police have only had calls from the usual freaks. Cashers-in on crime. Demanding impossible ransoms like half a million pounds. Or saying they've seen that gray Jag everywhere from Putney to Perth."

"Then the gray Jaguar was the kidnap vehicle?" Ella said uneasily. "As Mrs. Ingram calls it."

"Who knows? It's only a stolen car as far as the police are concerned. Look, love, this is nothing for you to worry about. Aren't you getting a bit of a thing about it?"

"I did have that odd telephone call."

"So you say."

"I *did,* Max. I told you."

"All right, all right, I'm not saying you didn't. Come and sit down and relax. What'll you drink? Have a gin and tonic. You look as if you need it. Where's Kitty?"

"In the garden. Sam's just gone home."

"Thank God for that."

"I filled the pool for them. They loved it."

"And what did you do?"

"Oh, I had Mr. Brontë over."

"Who?"

"You know. The Bramwells next door. He's Booth Bramwell, the theater critic. I've told you before."

"Then you don't mean Mr. Brontë, you mean Mr. Gin."

Ella laughed. Max wasn't usually so quick-witted.

"You must meet him. I think you'll find he's more a Brontë than a Booth's Gin. Actually, he's neither, really. He's not in the least highbrow to talk to. He says his sister would baby-sit if we wanted to go to the theater."

Max frowned, then had a second thought. "Now that just might be an idea. I've got to entertain some Germans from the Munich factory shortly. We could take them to a leg show. Just their cup of tea."

Ella thought, Why doesn't he ask me what I would like to see? Why doesn't he suggest that just the two of us have a night out? Why does all his thinking automatically turn to promoting business, promoting himself?

A night out with several fat German

businessmen roaring at prurient jokes was too awful to contemplate. It was so awful it was funny. She giggled as she sipped the drink Max had handed her, and he looked at her, thinking she was already getting a little high. She hadn't a very good head for alcohol. Usually he was less tolerant about it than he seemed to be this evening.

"Do you good, love. Make you relax. You've been on wires lately."

He was her husband, Ella was thinking. The man she had chosen to marry against all family advice. Not her kind, they had said. But he was hers now, the man she had shared everything with. They were part of each other, bound together, happy. Opposites made for success in marriage.

As long as one didn't have to love each other's friends.

It was clear already that Max wouldn't care for Booth Bramwell any more than she would for his foreign business associates.

"How did the meeting go?" she asked.

"Splendid. Smashing. The boss had some nice things to say about my trip."

"Oh, I'm glad. What about that poor Mr. O'Brien?"

"O'Brien?" His voice was so blank that one might have wondered if anyone called O'Brien existed.

"Darling! You accuse me of forgetfulness! The man in trouble last night."

"Oh, him." Max had moved on to new events, of course. O'Brien's problem was filed away.

"Don't mention that again, love. It's private between me and O'Brien. The boss doesn't know. I'm organizing moving him to the Midlands branch."

"Was it something dishonest he did?"

"Vaguely. Pity to sack the poor devil. Not to worry. It's not your concern. Have another gin?"

"Are we celebrating something?" She was usually not encouraged to drink more than one. "Your new job?"

"Not yet. Probably by the end of the week. Fingers crossed." Max reached for her glass. "Another drink will do you good. You're looking better already."

"I'm feeling fine."

"Well, you're still looking strained and worried. Not to be wondered at, the way your brain hasn't been functioning lately."

"Max! Not that again."

"Fact, darling. But you were all right today, weren't you? You were on time for Kitty and all that."

"*And* I drove carefully. Although someone behind me didn't. He nearly bumped into me. Deliberately."

A startled look jumped in Max's eyes, then was quelled, as he said with his new irritating concern, "You must have imagined that."

"It certainly looked like it. A horrid man. Sort of sinister."

"Ella! Get get out of your dream world."

"But it happened!"

"Kitty with you?"

"No, I was on my way to get her."

Max shrugged. No witnesses. My barmy wife is having another fantasy. She could read his mind as easily as she could read the inflections of his voice.

"Forget it," she said tiredly. "He didn't hit me, and I'm here safely. I'll go and get supper."

"Call Kitty in. It's too dark for her to be out."

"Max, it's broad daylight still."

"Well, it's late. I'm not keen on those fields at the bottom of the garden. Anyone can wander there."

"But, darling, the fields have always been there."

"And Kitty has only played outdoors alone this summer. She never left your side before that."

"I suppose so."

"I'm not thinking of her being kidnapped. God, I'm not rich enough. But you know what can happen to little girls."

Everything did come back to that kidnapping, Ella thought silently. Max had never been like this before, worried and uneasy. Sometimes Kitty might not have existed, for all the time he had to give to her. But now he seemed to be getting obsessions. It was he, not her, who seemed to be on the verge of a breakdown. Yet how could this happen within just twenty-four hours? It must be the result of the strenuous trip he had just made and his anxiety about getting the new job.

She went out to call Kitty, and could not see the little figure anywhere in the garden.

Panic struck her. Now she was catching Max's nervousness herself. She ran out, calling, "Kitty! *Kitty!*"

After a few moments Kitty appeared reluctantly from the tool shed, dragging the tumbledown perambulator behind her.

"Don't call so loud, Mummy," she complained. "You'll wake the family."

"Sorry, darling. I didn't think. It's time to come in. Daddy's home. He wants you."

But when they came in Max was speaking on the telephone. It must have rung while she was in the garden.

His voice was loud and emphatic. "Look here, I've done exactly — " Then he abruptly lowered his voice, as if he sensed Ella was listening. She could no longer hear what he said, although she thought she caught the words " — bloody lie! I gave you my absolute assurance. . . ."

It was that damn job again. Someone was needling him. It just wasn't worth it, if it was going to make Max live on tenterhooks all the time. It would be better to spend the rest of their lives in Collingham, in this tasteless house. She really could set to work to do something with it if she thought they were going to be here forever.

Actually it seemed a little more interesting now that the Bramwells had come to live next door. She had realized that ever since she had begun to watch Booth's dark head moving indistinctly behind the upstairs window and more now that he had visited and been so easy and friendly.

And of course another excitement was the discovery of the old house. That still had a certain dim enchantment at the back of her mind. She couldn't bear to leave Collingham until she had found out more about it.

"Who was it, Max?" she called, hearing the telephone ping.

He didn't answer, so she knew she shouldn't have asked. She got out plates and knives and forks and carried them into the other room.

"Kitty's in," she said. "She wasn't far away. Do you know, she got it into her head this afternoon to take Sam to see that old house."

Max, who had been slumped in his chair, as if brooding about that telephone call, shot his head up.

"You didn't let her!"

"That long walk after a day in school! Of course I didn't. Anyway, you know I wouldn't let them go alone. Perhaps at the weekend. And you could come, too."

She was astonished at his reaction.

"Ella, for God's sake, forget that crazy old house. It's making you dotty. I believe you dreamed up the whole thing. Even if it is there, this country's got too many rotting old houses, full of rats. There's nothing I want to see less. And don't talk to Kitty about it. I don't want her as dotty as her mother."

Ella's lip trembled. The gin, and now his unkindness, made her volatile emotions less controllable than usual. First he made her drunk, then told her she was mad.

"Is Daddy cross?" Kitty asked, her limpid eyes full of quick pain. Poor Kitty, to be born as ridiculously sensitive as her mother.

"He's tired, darling. That's all."

"By the way, Ella!" Max called presently. When she went in she saw that he

97

had had another drink, and was looking less strained.

"Yes, darling."

"If you were ever asked, I don't think I'd mention that house."

Ella frowned in bewilderment. "You've told me that before."

"And I'm telling you again."

"Who is likely to ask me?"

"I don't know. Anybody. I just don't want you talking about it. That screeching owl and the Edith woman. No one would take you seriously."

"Why? Because they'd think I was a bit gone in the head?"

"Putting it vulgarly, love, yes. I don't want people talking about my wife."

Slow anger stirred in Ella.

"Because it would prejudice you getting the new job?"

"Ella, what a thing to say."

"Otherwise you seem to have enjoyed my nuttiness. You can't keep off the subject." To her distress she heard her voice sharp and waspish. "You think it's rather a joke."

"It's far from a joke, believe me." Max saw her expression and said impatiently,

"Oh, forget it. You're so damn unpredictable. But just don't mention that house if you're asked what you were doing yesterday afternoon."

"Who on earth is going to ask me?" she demanded again. "The police?"

"I don't know. But if they've already traced the gray Jag to this area, who knows, they may start a house-to-house search. If they're taking this kidnapping seriously, they'll be pretty thorough. It'll be fingerprints next. Thank God I was on the plane."

"Max, you can't be serious!"

"Wouldn't look good, would it? Prospective export manager of large company has fingerprints taken."

"Honestly, Max — "

"Yes?" His eyes were hard, curiously hostile. "What were you going to say?"

"Nothing."

"You were, you know. You were going to say I never think about anything but my own selfish ambition."

"Well, do you?" she asked slowly.

"Of course I do. I think of your welfare. That's why I want a better job. And I'm scared the police might take your fantasies seriously."

"Fantasies?"

"You're repeating me like a parrot," he shouted, with a startling explosion of temper. "I said fantasies and I meant them. How could I expect you to sort them out from reality in your condition?"

"Con — " Ella began, and bit her tongue.

"You see," said Max wearily.

But all she could see clearly was that for some reason he didn't want to believe in the existence of that house. Or was she imagining that curious fact, too?

Kitty was devotedly putting her family to bed in the bottom drawer of the kitchen dresser. She kissed each shabby face tenderly. "Good night, Mary. Good night, Sue. Good night, Edith."

"You didn't used to have an Edith!" Ella said.

"Since yesterday I have. Rose is Edith Rose because she likes going to balls."

Ella, on the point of rushing in to Max with this evidence of Edith's existence, desisted. He would only say that Kitty repeated what her mother said. Parrot, he would say. And she was getting so confused, she was almost prepared to believe him. Perhaps she had dreamed the whole expedition yesterday, and Kitty was only repeating a long involved fairy story her mother had told her in the garden on a hot afternoon.

The owls, the rooks, the bees buzzing in and out of the purple foxgloves, the shimmering haze, the white butterflies like snowflakes. The wild flowers drooping in their bowl on the dining table!

"But Max, here's proof!" she declared, pushing the bowl under his nose.

He winced as a thistle scratched his chin.

"Robbing the hedgerows! Aren't there enough flowers in our own garden? Civilized ones."

"But you don't like me to pick them."

"Pick what you want to." His face had gone into that tight crinkling of temper again. "Just let's have some peace."

Again he didn't make love to her, which made two nights in a row, and this after a ten days' absence. It was unprecedented for Max, who had a keen sexual appetite, and a sure sign that he either wasn't feeling well, or was intensely worried about something.

Even when he slept, or appeared to sleep, his body seemed stiff and unrelaxed, and surely he was leaving her a generous two-thirds of the bed. Although it remained so hot and sultry during the entire night that there was no sense in increasing the heat by their bodies touching.

She had never felt less desire herself, but nevertheless would have welcomed Max's embrace, for the simple need of reassurance. All at once, inexplicably, he seemed to find her distasteful. He almost seemed to hate her.

If she were suffering, as he maintained, from that illness with the silly name, amnesia, she needed cosseting, not ostracizing. She shouldn't be allowed to lie awake worrying. If she didn't sleep she would be more vague and forgetful than ever the next day.

The midsummer moon shone through the window. She thought of its impartial light bathing the countryside, and the untidy garden around the old house, gleaming on the dusty dark windows, tracing the white flight of an owl. Then she began to wonder if it shone through any window on Mrs. Daphne Gibson with her long earrings, entwined secretly with her lover, or tied to a bedpost, trying to call out through the dirty rag that gagged her mouth.

Ella stiffened beneath the damp hot sheet. That last mental picture was extraordinarily vivid. And quite ridiculously melodramatic. Tied to a bedpost, indeed. Max was right. Her imagination was rioting out of control.

She fully intended not to mention the old house again, since it seemed to annoy him so much, probably as a symptom of the new strangeness of which he accused her. But the next morning halfway through breakfast she leaned forward, and the words came out of her mouth.

"Max, do come and see for yourself."

"See what?"

"That house. It's only an hour's walk. Or we might be able to find it from the road."

His face tightened, but he said quite mildly, "In case you don't remember, this is Tuesday and a working day. I'm due in my office at nine, and I have an appointment at nine thirty, followed by another at ten, and then I have to call on some customers. I'm a working man, love."

Tears were hot behind her eyelids. She was so tired, she felt she would like to weep for a long time.

"Don't be facetious, Max."

"I'm not being facetious, I'm merely stating facts. But maybe I'll relent. I might come on Saturday. Then we could take Kitty, too. If we can't find your ghost house we can have a picnic in the fields. How's that?"

Saturday seemed an immensely long way off, but she was grateful for that much of a concession from him. It had become absolutely necessary to show him the house in all its gloomy reality. Simply to prove her sanity, which he was holding in doubt.

She was feeling brainwashed about the whole thing. But this was only the result of two bad nights. She never felt close to reality when she was short of sleep.

Max threw down his napkin, and stood up.

"Now listen. The new car will be delivered about two. You will stay in, won't you? You won't forget."

"How could I forget an important thing like that?"

"Search me," said Max good-humoredly. "You'll have to collect Kitty in it, so get the man who delivers it to take you around the block once or twice for you to get the feel of it. Okay? You'll be able to manage, won't you?"

"Of course I will. You know I'm a good driver. That's why it was so odd about that telephone call yesterday."

Max scowled, then suddenly, surprisingly, took her in his arms and held her hard. That action more than anything emphasized his anxiety about her. She found it disturbing and wriggled away.

"Nothing will go wrong," he said, more as if he were reassuring himself than her.

"Of course it won't. I promise not to get your new car dented."

"Our new car."

No, it was his new car. It had been her new baby. She didn't suppose he saw it that way.

"Darling, ring me if anything happens. Leave a message if I'm out."

"You mean if the police come back?" Ella said instinctively.

"I don't think they will. There's nothing new on that missing woman in the paper this morning. She'll be getting nothing worse than divorce papers, you'll see. And she probably wants that. So why are we worrying about her?"

"I saw her with a rag around her mouth," Ella said involuntarily, then wished she hadn't because that suspicious look was back in Max's eyes, and she didn't need to be told what he was thinking. There was no need to feed his suspicions about her sanity. Besides, what *had* made her say that?

Max had been out of the house for less than five minutes before the telephone rang.

With a ridiculous feeling of apprehension Ella approached it. Thoughts raced through her mind. It could be Mrs. Ingram saying she was going to be late. Or her mother ringing from the country as she did once a week. But usually on Sunday. Or Sam's mother, asking her if she would pick Sam up this morning. Or even Booth Bramwell, by some unexpected chance.

But she knew, she knew. . . .

"And how are you feeling this morning, Mrs. Simpson?" came the common voice. "Better?"

"Who is that speaking?" she asked tensely.

She could hear breathing, but her question was not answered.

"Who *are* you?" she cried. "You have no business ringing me up like this. My husband — "

"Pay no attention to your husband, dear. If he cared about you he'd have you off to a doctor." There was a low snickering laugh. "But you pay attention to me, dear, because I care about you. You go and see a doctor."

The telephone clicked. Ella stood with the purring receiver clamped to her ear. She was as hypnotized as a rabbit by a rattlesnake. What could she do? She couldn't ring Max. He wouldn't be at the office yet. When he did arrive he had meetings. It would be impossible to get hold of him until midday at the earliest. Now it was time to take Kitty to school. And to drive carefully in case some careless driver was behind her.

As she at last put down the receiver and

looked at the silent innocent shape of the telephone she wondered if she were getting a persecution complex.

People with those, she had heard, were suspicious of everybody and everything. They swore things had happened that hadn't. Their mania came from a secret profound desire for love.

Max hadn't loved her at all, physically or in any other way, since he had come home two days ago. But two days were not sufficient time in which to induce in her a state of acute anxiety and deprivation. How absurd could she get? She pressed her hands to her temples as a shout rose up in her, *What is happening to me?*

The front door was open and the warm sunshine streamed in. Kitty, hair unbrushed, shoes untied, was sitting on the doorstep playing with her dolls. Ella looked at the clock and exclaimed guiltily. Now she was neglecting her own child.

"Kitty, bring your hairbrush and hair ribbon. Quickly, or you'll be late for school. You know Daddy doesn't like me driving fast."

Not Daddy. . . . That other mysterious

person who cares if I have an accident, who cares if I don't see a doctor. . . .

Why a doctor, for a bit of tiredness and muddleheadedness?

"Mummy, you're tugging!"

"Sorry, darling." Ella gathered the shining fine hair together and tied the ribbon with quick nervous fingers. "There. Let's go. And remember this afternoon I'll meet you in our new car. It's brown. Tobacco-leaf brown, I believe."

"Can Sam come in it?" Kitty asked inevitably.

"Oh, I expect so. If it's going to ruin your pleasure without him."

Nothing untoward happened on the drive to school, although Ella kept glancing in her driving mirror apprehensively. After she had dropped Kitty she had a great reluctance to go home as she was quite sure the telephone would be ringing. Then let it ring and ring and ring.

When Mrs. Ingram came she could answer it, and say that Mrs. Simpson was not available, unless the caller was Max.

Mrs. Ingram, when given these instructions, blinked her bright small eyes.

"Goodness, are you going incommunicado, Mrs. Simpson?"

Is she watching me, too? Ella found the sneaky thought taking possession of her as she saw the observant eyes, like jet beads.

"I'm feeling tired. My husband has insisted I have a quiet day. I'm going to sit in the garden in the shade."

"You do that, Mrs. Simpson. You are looking peaky, to be sure. It's this heat. Shall I carry a chair down the garden for you? Lucky it isn't Partridge's day, so you can sit where you want."

"Mrs. Ingram, if the telephone does ring, find out who's speaking. Make them give you a message."

"Don't I always do that, Mrs. Simpson? Well, I'd best get on. I'll bring you a nice pot of coffee and the radio."

"The radio?"

"You might like to listen to the news. Not that it'd cheer you up. Murders and kidnappings. I dessay that poor Mrs. Gibson has been raped or murdered by now."

"Mrs. Ingram!"

"Well, there ain't been no ransom note,

so what would they be doing with her, if it wasn't for money?"

Mrs. Ingram, with her apparently sophisticated knowledge of crime and the ways of criminals and police, had overlooked the fact that if there had been a ransom note it certainly could not be made public, otherwise how could the police lay a trap for the kidnappers? They would have to work in the utmost secrecy. Even at this minute they might be waiting concealed at some spot where the package of money was to be left. In a park perhaps, a hollow tree, or an unused shed, or an empty house.

An empty house! The thought flashed through Ella's mind like an electric spark. She immediately dismissed it. No need to get back to that obsession. There must be a million empty derelict houses in England. If the kidnappers should by any chance choose such a likely place for a rendezvous. They would be far more inclined to do something much less routine. Such as an isolated telephone box, a parked car. . . .

"Good morning, Ella. You look as if you're sunbathing on the French Riviera."

Booth Bramwell was leaning out of his

upstairs window. Was this going to become a habit of his? Ella decided she welcomed it. She had been feeling rather appallingly alone.

She waved, and said, "But my thoughts aren't Riviera thoughts."

"Oh, too bad. Tell me?"

"I was just wondering, if I were trying to get a large amount of ransom money, where I would ask for it to be left."

"Oh. And where would you?"

"Such an obvious place. An empty house. Like that one over there." She pointed into the heat-hazed distance.

"Aren't you thinking rather a lot about that old house?"

"That's what Max says."

"It's seized your imagination."

"Yes."

"I'd like to see it."

"Would you?"

"Why don't we walk over?"

For some reason Ella's heart began to pound.

"This morning?"

"Why not? I saw a bad play last night,

which should never have been staged, let alone deluding the public into paying to see it. It took me ten minutes to say so. Which was more time than it deserved. So I have a free morning, and you look as if you have."

Ella stood up uncertainly. "Max said he would come with me on Saturday. And Kitty wants to go again, and take Sam. With his gun."

"Saturday is a long way off."

"Why? Why do you say that?"

"The weather may not last. I'll be down in a couple of minutes."

But he hadn't been thinking of the weather, Ella knew. He had been thinking of ransom money, among other things. She knew he had. His mind worked in the same overcolored way as hers did. She felt relieved, and grateful not to be derided. What was more, her loneliness was leaving her.

She ran to the house, calling, "Mrs. Ingram! I'm going for a walk with Mr. Bramwell. We'll be a couple of hours, probably. Tell my husband, if he rings."

"With Mr. Bramwell?" said Mrs.

Ingram, her little mouth pursed.

"Mr. Brontë," Ella said gaily. "Max will understand."

Chapter 6

The moment they got into the fields away from the house Ella's spirits rose. A sense of freedom possessed her. She had escaped from the apprehension of the telephone, and from Max's recent peculiar tyranny. (If she were as strange as he insisted, shouldn't he be kind rather than hectoring?)

The undemanding but friendly companionship of Booth Bramwell, in his faded cotton sweater and sloppy trousers, was exactly what she needed.

She began to prattle, Kitty-wise.

"I'm so glad to get away from Mrs. Ingram this morning. She's full of that kidnapping. I really believe these disasters happen to give people like Mrs. Ingram delicious thrills. After all, they never get excited over someone's good fortune. That's too dull altogether."

"And what's her theory about Mrs. Gibson's kidnapping?"

"Oh, that she's been raped or murdered, or preferably both."

"She may be right. We live in violent times."

"I know. Will they pass or will they be worse when Kitty grows up?"

"Kitty will have her own aura of innocence to protect her. Like her mother."

Ella imagined that was meant to be a compliment, but because she had become so sensitive from Max's needling, she said flippantly, "I know I look trusting and gullible, but does that protect one? Mightn't it make me a victim?"

"What of?"

"Well, those peculiar telephone calls."

He stopped to look at her.

"What telephone calls?"

"It's silly. Max thinks I imagine half of it. There's this common sort of jeering voice saying be careful driving, and go and see a doctor."

"Is this true? I'm sorry, I do believe you," Booth added quickly, and she knew he did. "When did these calls come?"

"One yesterday afternoon and one this morning."

"Did the caller know who he was talking to?"

"Oh, yes. He calls me Mrs. Simpson."

"He'd get your name out of the book, of course."

"Perhaps. But why me?"

"Have you told your husband?"

"About yesterday, yes. Not about this morning because he had to be at meetings. We're getting a new car delivered this afternoon. Max thought the call yesterday would be someone from the factory telling me to be careful driving the car."

"Did he check?"

"No. He didn't take it very seriously. Nor did I, after I'd talked to him."

"But this morning was different. You were told to go and see a doctor?"

Ella swallowed. Her throat felt dry.

"This man said he was concerned about my health."

"Same voice as the day before?"

"Oh, yes, I'm sure."

"Do you think you should tell the police?"

"I don't know. I don't think Max would like it. I wouldn't go to the police without discussing it with him. Anyway, what could the police do?"

"They could tap your line."

"After only two funny calls?"

"Depends. It's damned unpleasant for you."

"I know. I was rather upset. I'd simply take the telephone off the hook, only Max might be wanting to get me."

"Why should someone be worried about your health?"

"I suppose because I haven't been well lately. I've been so absentminded and vague. It gets on Max's nerves."

"And on this other chap's?"

"But he's a stranger! He must be. I've never heard his voice before. Unless someone's playing a trick, disguising his voice."

"Do you have practical joker friends like that?"

"I hope not. Oh, let's forget it. I've probably imagined most of it. I mean, the sinister undertones. That's the sort of mind I've got. Fanciful. Offbeat."

"So Max says."

Ella looked at him reproachfully.

"I didn't say that."

He laid his arm across her shoulders.

"Sorry. Thinking aloud."

"You must meet my husband." Her voice, unintentionally, had become formal.

"I'm looking forward to it."

But they wouldn't like each other, Ella was thinking. The meeting wouldn't be a success. Max with his tense restless body, his thrust and energy, this man pleasantly lethargic, a little overweight, kind, seeing beneath the surface. They would have entirely different values. So what could they talk about?

If she liked to analyze the fact, she might find it disturbing that she seemed to find plenty to talk about to Booth Bramwell.

Once again the enchantment of the dark pathway emerging into the overgrown garden with its cloud of white butterflies, its untidy riot of color, possessed Ella. She looked quickly at Booth to see if he were similarly affected. As they came out into the sunlight, he stopped and stood still to gaze at the house with its blind windows, its look of utter desertion.

"You see, it does exist," Ella murmured.

"Of course."

"Wouldn't you like to live in a house like that? I would. So would Kitty."

"Let's go closer. I'd like to get inside."

"I don't think you can unless you break a window."

"Something must be unlocked. Let's test our burglar potential."

"I'll show you Edith's name scratched on the window. I told Kitty she borrowed her mother's diamond ring to write it, but now I think she used her own engagement ring. She probably loved her childhood home and wanted to put her mark on it before she had to leave it."

"Is that how you felt?" Booth asked, and again his perception disturbed her. She hadn't realized she had been thinking of herself and her recurring homesickness for her family home even after she had been married several years. Even still.

"But that's because we've had to live in horrid suburban houses until we can afford to get what we really want. Collingham was never meant to be permanent. Look, this is the window. You see. E-d-i-t-h.''

"Does it open?" said Booth.

It didn't. It was locked, or jammed from years of disuse. Strangely enough, in so derelict a house, every entrance seemed to be securely locked, even what was apparently the pantry window under a snarl of dank ivy.

"What are they shutting in?" Booth murmured. "The family jewels? The family skeletons?"

The blurred dirty windowpanes showed nothing but empty rooms, rotting floors, a glimpse of a winding staircase. The front door, set between slender Corinthian pillars, was as solid as the door to a prison, the stone steps mossy, the graveled drive overgrown with weeds.

"No one's been here for years," Booth said. "I wonder what the story is. Do you think I could climb up a drainpipe?"

"No!"

"I agree. I'm not the athletic type."

"Not that, but they'd collapse."

"More than likely."

"I hate laurels," said Ella. "Look at these specimens — covered in blight. In fact, I don't like the front of the house a bit. Let's go back to the garden."

"It seems a pity not to get in."

"What for? There's no one here."

"Which was the window the owl flew out of?"

"I'll show you." Ella led the way back to the terrace, and pointed to the high attic window. "That one."

"Then that's a strange thing."

"What?"

"The clever bird seems to have shut the window after it."

"It must have been the wind," said Ella, staring.

"Did the frame open outward?"

"I think so."

"Then it probably was the wind. Since there wouldn't conceivably be a strong draft inside the house with everything shut up. All the same" — Booth was frowning, and the queer titillating uneasiness stirred in Ella again — "you must admit there hasn't been much wind since the day before yesterday. Only this still heat.

"Unless it blew in the night," he added. "It would blow more out here, with all these trees. I must find out who this property belongs to and get the keys."

"They'll be rusty," said Ella, and they both began to laugh, relaxing from the uneasiness they each knew the other had felt. Ella sat on the sun-warmed stone of the terrace and breathed the hot scent of wallflowers.

"It's such a shame that a place like this should have gone to wrack and ruin. Perhaps there's a curse on it."

"More than likely. Listen to those crows cracking away about doom."

"They're rooks, and you're laughing at me."

"With you."

"Well, that's nicer. Sit down and tell me why you're not married."

"And what makes you think I'm not?"

"*Are* you?"

"I was."

"Oh." She wanted to ask him what had happened, but, seeing the closed look of his face, couldn't. "Do you still mind?" she asked at last.

"Of course. One dislikes failure. Personality failure. And don't look at me with those big eyes. Pools of innocence. As young as Kitty's."

"Don't be silly. I'm twenty-six. How old are you?"

"Thirty-three."

"And when did — I mean how long — "

"When did my wife leave me? Two years ago. My sister, who never intends to marry — she prefers books — thought our separation was an unmixed blessing. Among other things, she and I could set up house together proving that two can live more cheaply than one, more especially if the rule is applied to sisters rather than wives."

"Some wives."

"Sure. Some wives. Mine discovered that she preferred nightclubs to theaters, and my ink-stained fingers bored her. Which wasn't surprising. But it was a pity all the same."

"Incompatibility," Ella said.

"A nasty word. Still — water under the bridge."

"You were probably too kind to her."

"Me!"

"You have a nice slow voice."

"And that makes me kind? Mrs. Simpson, you're getting intuitions again. Next thing, you'll be conjuring up Edith to marry me. That's all I need, a neurotic virgin."

Ella laughed because it eased the awkward moment. She avoided looking into his unhappy eyes. She knew he didn't want her to see them.

"All the same," said Booth, changing the subject abruptly, "I don't believe we can go without getting inside this mausoleum. Let's commit an act of vandalism. If I break this pane of the French window I can put my hand in and turn the lock. Then we just walk in."

"No, don't!" Immediately Ella despised herself for her lack of courage and added recklessly, "All right, let's. Only you go first."

"We'll go together. You have to protect me from Edith."

A smell of mustiness floated out as the door creaked open. They tiptoed across the dry dusty floor toward the hall and the stairway.

"This was the ballroom." Ella realized she was whispering again. "And the next room the drawing room. Across the hall would be the dining room and perhaps a library. That passage would lead to the kitchen and scullery and stillroom and so on."

"You sound as if you'd lived here."

"It's like my old home. My parents still live there, and don't know what to do with all the space. Oh, I love this. It's so familiar. Look at the wallpaper. Cabbage roses. I'd say it was the original. Hung when Edith's parents built the house. Shall we go upstairs?"

"Of course. Mainly I want to see that attic room. Can you pick it out?"

"I think so. Be careful. There's a broken stair board here. Somebody heavy must have trodden on it. We'll have to go up two flights of stairs for the attics. I'm glad Kitty isn't here. She'd have been nervous."

"Aren't you?"

"Terribly. Look, that will be the main bedroom. It looks over the garden."

"Don't stop."

"Booth! You're nervous, too."

"No. Curious. This stair rail is sagging a bit. I wouldn't touch it. My God, this place would need a fortune spent on it."

"Are you thinking of buying it?"

"Not since you warned me about the curse."

Ella laughed, and heard her laugh echo. She shivered, although now her nervousness was rather enjoyable.

"No bloodstains," she said lightly.

"Not yet. Now, this is the top landing. The owl's room was the middle one, wasn't it?"

"I think so. It must be this one with the door shut. Booth! The door's locked!"

"Nonsense! It can't be!" Booth rattled at the handle, then set his shoulder to the door.

Again Ella heard herself whispering involuntarily, "Don't!" She was shivering again, less enjoyably.

But with a loud creak the door had opened.

"Only jammed," Booth said, and went inside.

The room was totally empty. Unless one could count a white feather in a corner, and some bird droppings.

"That owl!" Ella exclaimed.

"Sure enough. So that's what it was."

"What else did you think it might be?"

"Tramps. Hippies. This place would be a godsend to them if they discovered it. But it's too clean. They'd have left their usual trademark of debris." Booth was trying the window. It, like the door, was stuck. But only slightly. Suddenly it swung open, and a waft of delicious mild air came in.

"I suppose a sudden gust of wind could have done it," Booth was murmuring. "Well, there's your mystery cleared up."

"It was never really a mystery. All the same, I wouldn't like to be here alone. There's a sort of graveyard silence."

"It's your guilty conscience. We're trespassing."

"Yes, and heavens, look at the time! I've got to go. Max would never forgive me if I wasn't there to take delivery of the new car. He'd say my memory had failed again."

"You're not very enthusiastic about this car, are you?"

"We couldn't have afforded it if I hadn't lost the baby. So how can I be?"

Again he put his arm across her shoulders

as they walked down the creaking stairs. The gesture was better than his saying anything.

As they came into the empty ballroom an impulse seized Ella and she began to whirl around in a waltz. Then she leaned dizzily against the French window and said, "I'm mad. I love being mad."

"It suits you, Mrs. Simpson, my darling."

"I wonder where they had the orchestra and the potted palms. Is this good theater, Mr. Brontë?"

"It would be if anything happened. Pure Hitchcock if we'd found even a skeleton of a bird."

"Or a Victorian papa? At least, thank goodness, we've discovered one thing. The house is nothing to do with that kidnapping."

"Did you think it was?" he asked.

"Not really. I'm just mixed up. Can't separate fact from fantasy."

Outside again, the heat dazzled. Now it was the town of Collingham that was unreal, floating in haze, instead of this forgotten Victorian mansion. Ella felt her high spirits ebbing away as they came near the end of their long walk. What was waiting for her at home, and why was she dreading it?

It turned out, however, that there was nothing to dread. Mrs. Ingram had gone, leaving a telephone message carefully written out.

"Your doctor's secretary rang to say, Why didn't you keep your appointment yesterday? Will you ring and make another one?"

Ella grabbed her diary and checked. Relief sent her spirits bounding upward again. She had been due yesterday for her checkup after her miscarriage. She had completely forgotten about it but her forgetfulness was much less important than the fact that that queer telephone call this morning was explained. Or more or less. Someone had merely been reminding her about her forgotten appointment. Who it was, she didn't know, but she wasn't going to let that worry her anymore. She must merely have imagined that the voice was the same as the one from the car factory yesterday.

Although why should a man ring her, when her doctor's secretary was a woman? Miss Madden. She even remembered her name.

But, no, she wouldn't let that worry her. It was immaterial. At last she had something real to grasp, and was no longer lost in that woolly mystery.

The whole thing, as Max would say, was psychological. The lost baby and the new car had become mixed up in her mind to such an extent that she associated them both with danger. It was odd, but quite simple, really. She was sure Booth would understand.

Chapter 7

Mrs. Ingram had left another note on the kitchen table.

"You are low in butter and eggs, and you oughter use up that cold joint. I can't find no more coffee."

Snooper! But Ella decided fairly, she must need a snooper since a good housewife wouldn't run out of coffee, or throw out the remains of a perfectly good leg of lamb, as she was about to do.

Have to do shopping this afternoon, she thought. She should have done it this morning instead of spending that enthralling but wasteful time on the old house. Now she could only hope the car would be delivered on time, so that she could drive into the shopping center before picking up Kitty. Hopeless to keep Kitty and Sam, live sticks of dynamite, waiting in the new car while she queued in supermarkets.

"You ain't organized, Mrs. Simpson," Mrs. Ingram would say. But she had been saying that for months, not just since Ella's sudden vague state.

The vague state was certainly all too real, for she found it impossible to concentrate on what they should eat for supper tonight. Hot weather, therefore cold food. Salad, ice cream. Cold chicken? Max detested shop-cooked chicken. Why didn't Ella buy a bird and cook it herself?

Because she didn't feel like cooking today. She wanted to lie in the garden and dream.

So that was that. They would have cold chicken and ham, but she would toss a nice salad, and make chocolate sauce for the ice cream.

Anyway, it was too hot to eat.

At least the telephone hadn't rung. The house was blissfully quiet. She would ring Doctor Greave tomorrow. Better not tell Max she had forgotten that appointment.

And Max had said she could pick flowers

out of the garden, so she would. A huge bunch of delphiniums, carnations, roses and peonies. The living room would look like an expensive florist's shop.

Her mood, after the queer strain of the last two days, had flipped right over into happiness.

She wouldn't have noticed the parked car on the other side of the road unless the two men had been sitting in it.

They must be waiting for someone to come out of the house opposite. They sat very still, with their hats pulled low over their eyes. A couple of slim dark gangsters, she thought, George Raft style. She stood at the window, sipping her lunch, a glass of cold milk, and watching idly.

It was quite five minutes before her slow mind realized that they were watching her. Or this house. Their heads were definitely turned this way, and although occasionally they moved, and seemed to talk a little, they never took their eyes off the house.

She stepped sideways, behind the curtain. Her heart was bumping uncomfortably. If they wanted to see her or ask her questions, why didn't they come and ring the doorbell? Why did they just sit there staring with their indistinct eyes beneath their pulled-down hat brims?

What was it they wanted?

Their car was a dark-green Mini. One of thousands. Unmemorable, unidentifiable. She couldn't see the number plate.

It wasn't the sinister gray Jaguar, she told herself. There surely couldn't be anything especially significant about two men sitting talking in a very ordinary car. Just far enough away for her to be unable to recognize their faces. . . . Supposing that at some future date she was called on to identify them. . . .

The thought made her lean closer to the window to see more clearly, and at the same moment the telephone rang.

Ella found herself backing out of the room, unable to take her eyes off the watching men, reluctant to answer the insistent ring of the telephone. All the old ridiculous panic, from which after all she had not recovered, was back.

She finally picked up the receiver and answered in a breathless croak.

"Ella!"

It was Max. Relief was so profound that her legs trembled.

"I'm so glad it's you," she gasped.

"What's the matter?"

"There are two men in a car watching the house."

There was a longish silence. Then Max's voice came with an explosive sound. "Don't be mad! There can't be!"

"There are, Max! I tell you there are! They're wearing low hats like gangsters."

"I don't believe you. Where are they parked?"

"Across the road."

"Then they're calling at the Brewsters, of course."

"They're not, they're watching me through the front window."

"What's the number of the car?"

"I couldn't see."

"Then go and look again. Look through another window. Kitty's bedroom. That'll give you a side view."

"Yes, yes, I will. Hang on. Don't go."

She carefully laid down the receiver and raced upstairs.

Kitty's window looked onto an empty street. The car had gone.

She couldn't believe it. She clenched her hands in bewilderment and exasperation. She *couldn't* have imagined the car with its silent occupants sitting there. Yet the street, bathed in hot sunshine, was as innocent and silent as if nothing had passed down it for hours.

"It's gone," she said reluctantly to Max.

"Gone? You mean there's no car at all?"

"There was one, but it's gone now."

She heard him expel his breath in a loud sigh. Of relief?

"There *was* one," she insisted, forestalling his doubt.

"I'm not saying there wasn't, but what's funny about a car stopped for a few minutes across the road? Isn't that a perfectly normal happening?"

"It's just the way they were staring. The two men."

"Ella, darling! You're getting a persecution complex, do you know? You think you're being watched. Strange people are ringing you up. Classic symptoms."

"Classic symptoms of what?" she mumbled.

"Well, of an incipient breakdown. You've got to snap out of it."

Ella bit her lips. How could she tell Max about her earlier telephone caller now? Anyway, that had been Doctor Greave. Or someone. . . .

"How are things with you?" she asked in a subdued voice.

"Fine. Fine. I'm just off to lunch. I should be home in good time tonight. I want to take the car for a run. Don't forget, it's to be delivered at two o'clock. Stay in, won't you?"

"Of course I'll stay in. You've told me that a dozen times."

"Sorry, love. But it's necessary, the state of mind you're in. And do be careful driving."

"Not you, too!" Ella cried, stung to fury. "I've had enough advice, enough warnings! You'd think I was the village idiot."

"Sometimes not far off it," said Max with a strange little tolerant laugh, entirely unlike him.

So was that why he hadn't wanted to

make love to her lately? Because a village idiot surely couldn't have much sexual appeal.

Ella mopped at her tears. Honestly, she was crying as easily as Kitty, with her too tender heart, did. But all the calming Booth had done this morning was vanishing so rapidly. Her condition hadn't been cured, only temporarily alleviated. Now she was miserable with nerves and doubt again.

She had wanted to tell Booth about the watching car, asking him if he had seen it, but now she was afraid to mention it, in case she really had imagined it. Or that he, too, would think she was developing a persecution complex.

Of course it had been there. But whether the two men had been watching her — she supposed she could be convinced that she had imagined that. It would be better to try to forget it.

All the same, she hadn't imagined Max's relieved sigh when she had said they were gone — as if he really had been a little alarmed.

Or was that another tortuous turn her imagination was taking?

As I was going up the stair,
I met a man who wasn't there . . .

The foolish jingle rang in her head.

He wasn't there again today,
I wish that he would go away. . . .

But he had gone away. Or they had gone away. They had probably been television salesmen, or they were delivering samples of a new kind of soap flake, or frozen food, or whatever. They had merely been deciding whether hers was the kind of house and she the kind of gullible housewife whom it would be worthwhile to visit.

They had decided against it and driven away. Now everything was quiet and calm again, she could pick the flowers, and arrange them, then change into the kind of dress suitable for sitting behind the wheel of a smart new car.

It was such a perfectly ordinary day, one couldn't imagine sinister happenings.

For no reason at all, she wondered if Mrs. Daphne Gibson were sunbathing in some secluded garden, or on some anonymously crowded beach.

The Rover, tobacco-leaf brown, was driven by a freckle-faced tow-haired youth, who grinned at Ella in a friendly manner, and expected her to be wildly excited about her new possession.

"She's going nicely, Mrs. Simpson. Want to try her?"

"Yes, my husband said I had better drive with you around the block just to get the feel of it — her."

"You used to automatic drive?"

"Yes."

"Then there's nothing to it. Get in and I'll show you."

The car certainly went like a dream. With the young man sitting beside her, Ella drove around the block twice, and earned his commendation.

"You know how to handle her. You'll be fine, Mrs. Simpson. Got all your stuff out of the old one?"

"I think so."

"Okay. I'll take it and be off. Good luck."

Good luck. . . . Anyone needed that

driving on the roads as they were today. The young man didn't add, "Be careful driving," and he had gone before she remembered that she had been going to ask him if he knew who had telephoned her with that advice. She knew instinctively that he would have given her a blank stare of surprise.

Oh, well, forget it, and just *be* careful driving. Get your shopping basket and do the shopping before picking up Kitty. Park in the parking lot beside the supermarket, and take no notice of anybody.

She hadn't previously had this habit of talking to herself. Was that another sign of idiocy?

Of course it wasn't. She knew very well why she was doing it, because by saying words aloud, and constantly exhorting herself, her mind was occupied, and it couldn't worry and dwell on oddities. By hurrying out now to do her chores she got away from the telephone.

The heat had increased. Her white linen dress felt sticky and rumpled by the time she reached the school — safely, with her shopping done, and with no untoward occurrence — and parked at the curbside to wait for Kitty. The leaves of the plane trees lining the street looked faded and papery, the haze of heat and gasoline fumes made the air misty. The new leather of the car seats smelled too strongly. Ella felt suddenly dizzy, a combination of heat and lack of a solid lunch making the day blur. She closed her eyes for a moment, and when she opened them the long face, anonymous behind very large dark glasses, was looking in at her.

She gasped, and the face drew back, turned sideways.

In case she should stare at it too closely, memorize it? But what could she see except the black stare?

"You okay, lady? Thought you looked sick."

"I'm perfectly all right, thank you."

"Fine. Kids are coming out now."

He was walking away, showing a long narrow back, a narrow head with sleeked black hair curling at the ends.

"Are you waiting for your child?" she called.

But he didn't answer. He continued walking away, so it was obvious that he was not waiting for a child, obvious also that he knew she was, and that probably he knew *who* she was.

But couldn't he have been just an ordinary passerby, concerned that the driver of a smart new car was looking pale and ill? Or had his voice been faintly familiar?

What was the use? she thought despairingly. She no sooner induced in herself a state of not-caring lethargy, and she was jolted back into this black muddle of doubt and bewilderment again.

A persecution complex, Max had said. The man with the long unhurried stride was in the distance now, becoming lost in the heat haze. He hadn't even turned back to see what that poor muddleheaded Mrs. Simpson, who should see her doctor, was doing next.

Kitty and Sam erupted out of the school gates.

Sam exclaimed, "It's a super car, Mrs. Simpson."

"Yes, well, be careful of it. No dirty boots on the seats. No sticky fingers."

"It's tobacco-leaf brown," said Kitty smugly. "I like that better than gray."

"Why gray?" Ella asked.

"The gray Jag," said Kitty. "Mrs. Ingram's always talking about the gray Jag."

"That's the robbers' car," said Sam.

"Robbers! What are you talking about, you silly little boy?"

"They're bank robbers, my father said. Or kidnappers. They've got guns."

"So have you," said Kitty admiringly. "Sam always brings his gun, Mummy. He says you never know when you'll need it."

"I think Sam has an overdeveloped imagination," said Ella, driving carefully, turning the purring new car toward home.

"Gosh, Mrs. Simpson!" Sam exclaimed.

"What is it now?"

"That's a police car at your house!"

It couldn't be. It must be another example of Sam's lurid imagination. But it was a police car, and there were two policemen sitting in it, waiting for her.

She stopped beside them, and got out of the car slowly.

"What is it? Have I done something wrong?"

"Nice car, ma'am."

"Yes, and it's registered, and I have my driving license and I didn't park on a double yellow line, or break any speed limits."

"You lady drivers, you get a guilt complex," said the sergeant, grinning. "This call is nothing personal. We're only making some more inquiries about — "

"The gray Jaguar?"

"Not exactly. Only whether you're quite sure you didn't see anything unusual on Sunday afternoon. What were you doing, by the way?"

Ella frowned, trying to remember. Really, her memory! It seemed so long since Sunday. That was when Max had returned from abroad, of course. Oh, and she and Kitty had discovered the old house.

But Max hadn't wanted her to talk about that. He said it made her seem crazy.

"Sunday," she said vaguely. "It was hot. My daughter and I went for a walk across the fields at the back of our house. We picked wild flowers. That was all."

"What time was this, and how long were you away?"

"Oh, I'd say from about three o'clock till six. I was expecting my husband home from abroad, so we got back in plenty of time. He arrived about seven o'clock. Is that what you wanted to know?"

One of the men was making notes in a little book.

"That's all you can tell us, Mrs. Simpson? You didn't see anything out of the ordinary on your walk?"

"Nothing at all." (Would one call a derelict house something out of the ordinary?)

"Thank you, ma'am. Sorry to trouble you."

The men got back into their car. Ella said compulsively, "Am *I* the only one being troubled?"

"Good gracious, no, Mrs. Simpson. We're doing a house-to-house inquiry."

"It's about that kidnapping, isn't it?"

"Could be."

"Then it *is* a kidnapping!"

"Time will tell, Mrs. Simpson."

"Then, for goodness sake, what do you imagine I have to do with it? Or Max?"

"Max?"

"My husband. He's in the city all day. He

had just got back from Germany that night. I told you."

"No need to get upset, ma'am. We have no reason to suspect your husband."

The car backed out of the drive, and whooshed off. And of course they had no reason to suspect Max, how fantastic could her imagination get? Yet the thought had been put into words, so now there was another worry to whirl about inside her brain.

For heaven's sake, Max didn't even know Mrs. Daphne Gibson! Or did he? How did she know whom he knew? Mr. Gibson was a rich businessman. Successful businessmen moved in small intimate circles, just as doctors, lawyers, artists, did. They used the same clubs, attended the same functions. . . . Perhaps Max did know the attractive Mrs. Daphne Gibson with her dangling diamond earrings.

He had certainly traveled back to England by air last Sunday, but supposing he had caught an earlier plane than he had told her. Then he had had that odd upsetting telephone call that had sent him hurrying out again, soon after arriving home. Last night he had had another one, and he had called someone a bloody liar and come in looking yellow.

He had scarcely touched her, let alone made love to her since he had come home.

Oh, God! Ella cried silently. Am I truly crazy? And saw Kitty watching her with those enormous anxious eyes of hers, and quickly said, "It's nothing, darling. Only routine inquiries. The police won't be back. Now what are you and Sam going to do?"

"Play kidnappers," said Sam inevitably, brandishing his gun. "I'll kidnap your family, Kitty, and you can pay me two pounds to get them back."

"You mustn't be unkind to them!" Kitty cried.

"You'll play no such thing," Ella said sharply. "I'll fill the pool. You can play in that."

But she had remembered not to mention the empty house to the police. Max would be pleased about that.

Why?

Booth, looking over the back fence, called, "Got your car?"

"Oh, yes. It's fine. I picked Kitty up. No accidents. The police were waiting when I got back. Did they call on you?"

"Yes. Just routine."

"I know. That's what they said."

"Lorna and I spent last Sunday with friends in Richmond, so we were out of all this excitement."

"What *was* the excitement?"

"Apparently that gray Jaguar they're asking about came down this street, traveling pretty fast. They seem to think Mrs. Gibson may have been in it. Someone thinks they saw a woman struggling."

"How do you know this? I haven't been told a thing."

"I'm in newspapers, remember? I have my sources. It's suspected that there's been a genuine ransom demand."

"Really!"

"Don't say I told you. It won't be made public yet. And don't look so worried!"

"Will the husband pay what they ask?"

"I daresay some arrangements will be made."

"So it will soon be over. They'll be caught."

"One hopes so."

But they would be too clever to be caught. Ella knew that quite certainly.

Chapter 8

Max didn't get home early after all. Ella found herself getting jittery listening for him. She had sent Sam home long ago, and Kitty had finally been persuaded to go up to bed if she were allowed to drag the family, rickety pram and all, up the stairs.

"But they always sleep in the kitchen," Ella said.

"It isn't safe any longer," Kitty said earnestly. "They might be kidnapped."

"Now what *ever* makes you say that?"

"Because of that lady Sam told me about."

"And who told Sam?"

"The police. They asked him if he'd seen the gray Jaguar with the screaming lady in it."

"Not Sam! Not a little boy! Anyway,

that's a terrible exaggeration. A screaming lady."

"He listened to what they said," Kitty said ambiguously. "That's why he never goes anywhere without his gun now. He wants to marry me," she added, imparting the information in a careless way, "so he can protect me."

"And don't you think your parents can do that?"

"At school?" said Kitty, with her sudden alarming intelligence. "When you're not there?"

What was this, an indoctrination into fear? Now even Kitty was doing it to her, suggesting that school wasn't safe. Just as Max had kept insisting on her seeing Kitty safely through the school gates in the morning, and out of them in the afternoon.

"Sam's a silly little boy who watches too much television," Ella said with asperity. "I hope you told him you had no intention of marrying him. And what could possibly happen to you at school?"

"I told Sam we heard a scream, too," said Kitty. "He said I was making it up."

"Yes," said Ella slowly. "That's what

Daddy said. Anyway, you know very well it was only that owl."

"All the same" — Kitty was carefully parking the dilapidated perambulator beside her bed — "if my family was going to be kidnapped I would have to take them away and hide them."

That word was being used far too often. It was like one of those subtle poisons that slowly and insidiously affected people's minds. Even five-year-old Kitty had caught the disease.

"The important thing," Ella heard herself saying in a quiet and normal voice, "is never to speak to a strange man, or get into a car if he asks you. I've told you that before, haven't I? It's very important. Tell your family."

Kitty could be trusted to regard as important anything that might affect her family's welfare. It seemed an underhand way of impressing on her something that had, over the last two days, become so strangely vital. Ella found herself ridiculously counting the number of tousle-headed or bald heads in the perambulator, and announcing all were present and correct, even down to the clothespin doll she had tied up in a shawl for Kitty one rainy afternoon two years ago, and which was still lovingly cherished.

She kissed Kitty's brow, looked at the serene little face, untouched by the conversation with its undercurrents of fear, told her to undress and brush her teeth, and Daddy would come up later.

It was as she went downstairs that the flap of the letter box rattled. Twice, as if someone were trying to thrust some too large object in.

She stopped still, waiting for the doorbell to ring.

It didn't, and nothing fell through the letter box.

By the time she had got her stiff legs down the stairs, and persuaded her reluctant fingers to turn the doorknob and open the door, there was no one there.

The warm evening air flowed in. The path to the gate was empty. The sweet peas climbing the trellis needed watering, Ella noticed with the part of her mind that still functioned normally. Max would be sure to tell her that she should have done it. Or that he had especially told her to do it.

Perhaps he had. She couldn't be sure. She only knew that nothing would induce her to stay out there in the slowly darkening evening where she could so easily be watched. Not by her neighbors, all of whom she knew by sight, but by the person who had just rattled the letter box to deliberately frighten her, and was now watching elatedly from some place of concealment. Someone with a perverted sense of humor, or worse.

Footsteps approached down the street. Ella was hesitating on the edge of flight indoors, when a shortish plump dark-haired woman appeared.

Lorna Bramwell, Booth's sister.

"Hullo, Mrs. Simpson. Enjoying the evening?"

"I'm waiting for my husband."

"Is he coming by train? Only person I met was my brother on his way into town. Poor devil, having to sit in a theater tonight, with no air conditioning. He says I needn't criticize theaters when I think of the rabbit warren of the London Library."

Had Booth just gone by?

But he wouldn't do that flippant

mischievous letter-box rattling.

What was happening to her, that she was so suspicious of everybody?

"It is hot, isn't it?" she said feebly.

"You're telling me! By the way, Booth said something about baby-sitting. If you and your husband want an evening out, I'd be glad to."

"Thank you. That's very kind. Actually we don't go out much."

"You ought to." The face looking at her was middle-aged, plain, honest, intelligent. A good face to turn to, Ella thought irrelevantly, if you needed sympathy or reassurance.

"You're much too attractive to be hidden away. I agree with my brother."

"Oh — did he — "

"My ex-sister-in-law was just the opposite to being a stay-at-home. She never was at home. There's a happy medium."

"I suppose there is. Actually, when my husband gets his new job — I mean, if he does — I'll have to do quite a lot of entertaining. Pull myself together," she added, humorously self-deprecating.

Lorna Bramwell's keen black eyes,

remarkably like her brother's but less attractive in a woman, stared at her.

"Do you need to?"

"Oh, yes. I have a stupid habit of daydreaming."

"Psychological."

My bird brain doesn't understand what you mean by that. Ella would like to have called some such remark after Lorna Bramwell's superior back. But already her pernicious daydreaming was comparing the dullness of a wife who was always at home to the exasperation of one who never was.

Did the ex-Mrs. Booth Bramwell disappear with other men (as Mrs. Daphne Gibson, reputedly kidnapped, obviously did)? And did she leave notes for her husband to find when he returned from his theater stints? Even if she didn't care for the theater it wouldn't be absolute purgatory to wait up for her husband with drinks and a little pleasant supper prepared.

Ella was jerked out of her reflections as arms folded around her waist. She screamed and struggled wildly.

"Shut up! Don't be such a little idiot! It's only me," said Max.

"But where did you come from?" Ella gasped, pushing his hands away. She had suddenly felt desperately imprisoned.

"I was in the garage looking at the car. You were too busy talking to Miss Gin. I beg your pardon, Miss Brontë."

"Max, don't be so silly. Actually, she seems rather pleasant."

"Getting very pally with your neighbors all at once, aren't you? You've never bothered before."

"It's just happened. I don't know. It's the hot weather, I think. We're out of doors more. But I didn't see you come in. It wasn't you who rattled the letter box, was it?" she demanded suspiciously.

"And then rushed and hid in the garage? Don't be so ridiculous. *Did* someone rattle the letter box?"

"I thought so," Ella said uncertainly, shaken already by his now-too-familiar skeptical look. "Yes, someone did," she added defiantly. "That's why I came out. I thought someone was playing a trick on me."

"Now why exactly would someone do a crazy thing like that?"

"Schoolboys," said Ella. "Sam, maybe. But I sent him home a long time ago."

Max laid his arm across her shoulders.

"Come on in, love. It's nothing to get upset about, even if it did happen. This is the wrong end of the day for you lately, isn't it? You get tired and overwrought. I say, the car's rather smashing. How was it to drive?"

"Fine."

"Hey! I'd like a little more enthusiasm. A man who buys an expensive car for his wife to go shopping in!"

"I didn't ask for it," Ella said, and knew she was being ungracious and ungrateful.

It should have been our baby, Max. Why don't you care about that?

"I know you didn't. And you're looking like a girl who's had a long day. What are we eating? Hot or cold?"

"Cold."

"Good. Then we can take time over our drinks. I'm sorry I was late. The boss wanted to see me, just when I was leaving."

"Oh."

"Aren't you going to ask me what about?"

She knew by his triumphant expression what it was about. Yet there was something uncertain and uneasy beneath his triumph.

It wasn't like Max to be uncertain.

"They haven't decided on the job already, have they?" she said dutifully.

"No. But apart from formalities, you know, courtesies — well, that's what I was given to believe. It's going to be announced by the end of the week. Three more days."

"That isn't long."

"Seems like forever to me."

Ella saw the lines of stress around Max's mouth and eyes, and knew he was speaking the truth. She must be an imperceptive wife not to have realized how much this job meant to him. Much too much in terms of tension. But Max wouldn't see it that way. He accepted the fact that the price of success was in terms of stress and tension. That was how he was made.

"By the way," he was saying, "the boss is giving a dinner party next Tuesday after the announcement is made. Whether I'm the winner or the loser, we'll have to be there. I want you to get yourself something to wear. Go into the West End. Find something special. You see, it's turned out lucky after all that you're not heavily pregnant."

A smart new car, a fashion-plate wife, preferably sterile. . . . Had these always been Max's values?

No, she was being unfair. If she expected him to understand her, she must also understand him, and his deep compulsive hungers.

"Cheer up, love. Aren't you pleased that I'm proud of you — when you're not looking so vague and worried?"

"Am I?"

"Yes, you are, and you've got to snap out of it by next Tuesday. Nothing else worrying you — apart from those cranky telephone calls?"

"The police came again," she said, and was startled by the quick irrepressible alarm in his face.

"What did they come for?"

"Only to ask more questions about Sunday. Anything I might have seen, what I was doing."

"And you told them?"

"That Kitty and I found that old house? No, I didn't mention that. You told me not to." Besides, it was secret, she didn't want the police's heavy hands on her dream. Booth Bramwell, practically a stranger, she suddenly realized, was the only person with whom she could share the dream.

"It's irrelevant," Max muttered.

"Irrelevant to what?"

"To what they're getting at, of course. The gray Jaguar."

"You said it would make me seem crazy."

"All that Edith nonsense. You're damned right it would."

"You think the firm wouldn't give you the job if they knew you had a — an unbalanced wife?"

"Not unbalanced. Just tired. Run-down. No, of course they wouldn't let that stand in my way. They're decent humane people. But I'm vain enough to want them to see you at your best."

That was one of the things this women's liberation campaign was about, that a woman shouldn't just be an asset, a chattel, to a man. But if one loved him — and she did love Max, didn't she? — one wanted desperately to be an asset, at least.

"So you told them you hadn't seen anything significant," Max was saying, reverting to what he regarded as the more important subject.

"Yes. I told them that. I said Kitty and I had gone for a walk across the fields at the time the gray Jaguar was supposed to have passed. They seemed to think that kidnapped woman was in it."

"Maybe she was. But of her own free will. I don't go along with a kidnapping."

"But there's supposed to have been a ransom letter, only it's being kept secret."

Max, at the sideboard pouring drinks, turned sharply.

"How do you know?"

"Booth — Mr. Brontë — I mean Mr. Bramwell, told me."

"How does *he* know?"

"He's on a newspaper, Max. He hears things."

"Well, tell him to keep them to himself and not to alarm my wife."

"I'm not alarmed," said Ella. "I'm not even surprised. I always thought Mrs. Gibson was kidnapped, simply because nowadays it's always the worst that happens."

"Well, for being an optimist — "

"A realist."

"You! My little addlepated wife a realist?" Max burst out laughing, with an edge to his laughter that Ella didn't care for. Or was she imagining that, was it part of this persecution thing he said she was suffering from?

The ringing of the telephone cut like a guillotine across Max's amusement. He stood a moment rigid, the whiskey decanter in his hand.

"I'll get it," said Ella.

"No."

That was the second time he had forbidden her to answer the telephone. So he must believe what she had told him about those funny calls. . . .

What was more, he closed the door between the living room and the hall. He didn't even want her to hear what he said!

Shamelessly she put her ear against the keyhole.

"Yes," she heard him saying in a taut voice. "Everything is under control. I give you my word. Now look here, cut it out. . . ." Ella heard the rising anger in his voice.

There was a long silence as he listened to his caller. Then, surprisingly, he said in a mild, almost a humble voice, "Yes, sure, but for how long? . . . You said yesterday . . . I guess so . . . I guess I can wait that long . . ."

The bell pinged as he hung up, but he didn't come back into the living room. After a few minutes, when Ella went to look for him, he called in a muffled voice from the downstairs washroom, "For God's sake, Ella! Can't I even have a wash!"

"Is everything all right?" Ella asked anxiously, as he emerged.

"What do you mean by everything?"

"That was someone from the office bothering you again, wasn't it? Tell me, Max, is someone jealous of you?"

He seemed to grasp her suspicions with relief.

"Of course. That's a built-in factor in competitive business."

"Who is it?"

"Never mind. You don't know him."

No, she didn't, and she didn't want to, but if that call had been from a jealous confederate, why was Max so meekly agreeing to do exactly what he asked?

That thought came later, when she realized that Max had been lying to her. He had some secret worry which he wanted to conceal. And he was using irritation with her as a red herring.

He had suddenly noticed the bowls of flowers and was exclaiming indignantly, "Ella! Whatever made you strip the garden like that?"

"But you told me I could. You said you didn't like wild flowers."

"Now, Ella, you know I did nothing of the kind! You know I won't have the garden spoiled. What's Partridge going to say tomorrow? Anyway, they smell like a funeral indoors."

"You told me I could pick them," Ella repeated. "Honestly, it's not me who's being forgetful, it's you."

"Hardly, love. Hardly. When have I ever allowed my flowers to be picked. All my delphiniums, my peonies!" He was touching the cut flowers, and seemed almost about to weep, as if this final trivial happening were unendurable.

But he *had* told her she could pick them. Hadn't he . . . ?

It certainly was true that he had never before allowed his precious flowers to be picked. It was something he was eccentric about, as she very well knew.

So had she imagined his permission?

"Well, never mind," he was saying more kindly. "I suppose I can't blame you, since you have this amnesia. You've simply got to get over it. You'd better go and see Doctor Greave."

You go and see a doctor, Mrs. Simpson. . . .

"I intend to, " she said meekly.

"Good. Then let's relax and behave like ordinary people."

But ordinary people didn't keep looking at each other with sidelong suspicious glances. Or make such polite stilted conversation. Or lie in bed carefully not touching each other, pretending it was because of the heat.

It was as much her fault as Max's, Ella admitted fairly, because she too was

168

becoming secretive. Apart from keeping silent with the police, she knew she had never intended to tell Max of her visit with Booth Bramwell to the old house.

He simply wouldn't understand the compulsion that had taken her there, and he would make unsympathetic remarks that would destroy the remembered pleasure of the morning.

What was this cold lonely thing that was happening to them?

Ella moved.

"Max? Are you asleep?" She knew he wasn't.

"No."

"I'm sorry about picking the flowers. I must have misunderstood you."

"It's all right."

"Don't just forgive me because you think I'm sick!"

"Oh, Ella. It's late. I'm tired."

"Max, what's gone wrong? You're behaving as if you don't even like to touch me."

"In this heat? God, this house is airless."

"The windows are all open. Anyway, I'd always heard that Latin races are more passionate because of the heat.''

"What's that got to do with it? I'm not a Latin!''

Ella laughed and rolled toward him. She didn't want to make love herself. She was too tired and too tense, but she had to establish what had changed Max's very fixed behavior patterns.

"I know you're not. But you always — ''

"Make love when I come home from a trip? Sure. I know what you're getting at. Sorry, love. I've got too much on my mind. Not in the mood.''

"It isn't me?'' Ella asked cautiously.

"With your funny old amnesia? Well, I like you better when you're with it, I admit. Not to worry.''

He patted her heavily on her thigh, and she, reassured by this more natural and friendly gesture, said, "I got the stupid feeling today that you might know that woman.''

"What woman?''

"Mrs. Daphne Gibson.''

Max turned violently, making the bed creak.

"Now what on earth — Oh, God, Ella, you are bats!"

Why had she said that? *Why* had she? Now the doubtful peace was wholly lost.

"I've never set eyes on her in my life," came Max's tight furious voice. "The next thing, you'll be accusing me of having an affair with your precious ghostly Edith. Honestly, the sooner you get to a doctor the better."

"I don't know why I said that," Ella confessed miserably. "It's only that all our troubles seem to have begun with that kidnapping."

"Wrong, love." Max was calmer now. Had his reaction been too violent? "They started with your trauma about that old house and the owl and whatever. You've never been the same since. You've developed this thing about people ringing you, people watching you, people playing tricks on you with the letter box. God knows what it will be next."

"It's all been the truth."

"I expect you think so. Promise to discuss it with Doctor Greave. If he suggests a headshrinker — "

"A psychiatrist!" Ella exclaimed. "Max, you don't believe I need one of those."

"I hope you don't." His lips rested momentarily on her bare shoulder. The little embrace seemed almost furtive. Then he turned over, the conversation finished.

Ella turned over, too, away from him, and silently wept.

It was unbelievable that the heat should go on. It was as if one day hadn't come to an end, with the blurred burning sun, the heat-hazed distances, the sticky smell of gasoline fumes and melting tar on the streets, the warm unstirring air, before the next had merged into it, making it one day of limitless hours.

Even Kitty was looking washed-out, her eyes enormous, delphinium blue, in her pale face. Ella avoided the mirror herself. She quessed the havoc another bad night would have played on her face. She made herself be busy and cheerful, so that Max would not be provoked into more remarks about her seeing a doctor. His attention, however, was given to the late arrival of the morning paper. He was muttering angrily about that,

172

and when it did come at last, he snatched it up as if the news, or some particular item, were vital to him.

Within a couple of minutes he had tossed it away, looked at his watch and said he would have to fly. The tension lines were sharply back around his mouth.

"But you've had nothing but a cup of coffee, darling."

"Who wants to eat, in this weather? Don't fuss, Ella. Penny will get me a sandwich later."

"Sandwiches! Starch!"

"Nothing wrong with my figure," Max said, more amiably. He was vain about his lean good looks, and liked to be reminded of them.

"I was thinking of your digestion. Aren't all top executives ulcer material?"

He patted her shoulder. He was looking more like himself. "I'm not a top executive yet, love. Keep your fingers crossed for me."

Then it was all spoiled by the now familiar litany. "Be careful taking Kitty to school. Don't be late for her this afternoon. If you do get any wrong telephone numbers don't get into a state about it and think someone is persecuting you."

"Don't open the door to strange men," Ella murmured, and Max took her up sharply on that. "I certainly hope you wouldn't be so foolish."

"Max, I'm getting tired of this village idiot treatment."

"When you stop deserving it, love, you'll stop getting it."

Did he mean that to be a joke? Or as unkind as it sounded? He wasn't looking at her, so she couldn't see whether he was being funny or not. It seemed a long time since he had worn his comical leg-pulling expression, one she was rather fond of, even if the jokes were at her expense.

He didn't seem to like to look at her much at all, lately.

Since returning home on Sunday. That was the exact time that this had started.

And perhaps it genuinely was her fault. Perhaps she was odd and unreliable and exasperating. After all, how would she know if her memory had got so bad?

Chapter 9

"Lor, all them flowers!" exclaimed Mrs. Ingram. "Whatever did Mr. Simpson say?"

"I felt like picking them," Ella said airily, not intending to discuss that little contretemps with Mrs. Ingram.

"Ever so gay," Mrs. Ingram murmured, but thinking something else entirely, Ella was sure. "That'll give Mr. Partridge a surprise."

"They aren't his flowers, Mrs. Ingram."

"No, but he thinks so. Did you get some coffee, Mrs. Simpson, like I told you?"

"Yes, and there's some on the stove if you can bear to drink hot coffee in this weather."

"Good! I'm ravaged for it."

Sometimes Mrs. Ingram's malapropisms made Ella smile. But not today. It was very unsmiling weather. Or should one say climate? A climate of violence, of strikes, of protests, of greed, of deceit, of fear. . . . A truly unsmiling climate.

"Well, cheer up, Mrs. Simpson. At least you ain't held in duress."

"In what?"

"Like Mrs. Gibson. That's what the paper says."

Ella snatched up the paper, seeing in her action an exact similarity to Max's earlier.

Had he been looking for news of Mrs. Gibson whom he swore he didn't know?

There it was, a small item, but on the front page.

"It is now almost certain that Mrs. Daphne Gibson, wife of wealthy industrialist Bernard Gibson, missing from her luxury Surrey home since Sunday, is being held under duress. Police are urging anyone who may have seen or heard anything significant on Sunday afternoon, especially in the vicinity of Collingham, Surrey, to get in touch with their local police station. They would particularly like to trace a gray 1966 4.2-liter Jaguar which is known to have been stolen. There have

176

been several telephone calls demanding ransom, but these are believed to be hoaxes."

"They wouldn't talk about the one that wasn't a hoax," said Mrs. Ingram, with her surprising insight into the ways of the police. "They'd work on that quietly, wouldn't they? Lure the kidnappers into a trap."

"I should think they'd be too clever to be caught."

"Not after they get cocky. And they will get cocky when they start feeling safe. If it isn't too late, of course."

"Too late?"

"Stands to reason they can't keep a lady like her fed and quiet for too long. She looks the kind that'd put up a fight, don't she? Not like a baby that can't say a word. Even someone as old as your Kitty would be potential dynamite." Mrs. Ingram liked the sound of those words. "I don't see as how they can ever let Mrs. Gibson go, while there's breath in her body, ransom or not."

Partridge arrived then, clumping down the paved path to the garden, and Mrs. Ingram, to whom all men were a welcome diversion, bobbed out of the back door to speak to him. Ella saw them looking at the denuded garden, and then toward the house, as if the walls were invisible, and they were staring at her standing guilty and defenseless in the living room surrounded by the bowls of plundered flowers. Partridge's large red face wore a look of baffled astonishment. Mrs. Ingram said something, gesticulating, and he slowly nodded, then slowly shook his head, as if in deep concern.

Poor Mrs. Simpson, they were saying, she isn't very well, she does odd things, and forgets. Is it likely Mr. Simpson would have told her she could pick all his precious flowers, you know how he likes to see them blooming in the garden?

Ella made herself open the French windows and step outside.

"Good morning, Partridge. Don't look so distressed. I didn't pick all the flowers. There are plenty of buds."

She was not going to defend herself. She was not going to say, "My husband told me I could." Besides, they were her flowers just as much as Max's. Marriage was sharing, wasn't it? (But not thoughts, not the secret worries that kept Max tense on his side of the bed, unrelaxed even when sleeping. . . .)

The two pairs of eyes stared at her, Partridge's accusing, Mrs. Ingram's sharp and knowing.

Ella opened and closed her damp hands. If she now thought she was being watched by her domestics, she really was getting this persecution thing. She said with asperity, "Mrs. Ingram, this won't get the work done. I thought we'd clean the windows today, while the weather's so fine."

Not lying in the garden in the shade thinking too much, but working hard, exhausting herself, so that her mind became numb.

When the telephone rang she knew that Mrs. Ingram, on the outside of the French windows, with a broom and a bucket of water, was straining to listen. But didn't she always, even when the calls were innocent?

Now they were no longer innocent.

Before he spoke, Ella could hear the deliberate exaggerated breathing.

Then her persecutor said, "Hi, Mrs. Simpson. Nice morning."

She exploded, "Look, if it's you again,

I'm just warning you that I've reported you to the police."

"No, you haven't, Mrs. Simpson. You're too scared to. And how right you are."

"Why?" she demanded with all the belligerence she could muster.

"Because if you do I'll report your husband for that mink jacket he smuggled through customs the other day. Ask him about it, Mrs. Simpson. Ask him who it was for."

Now she was wordless. She listened helplessly while the hateful mocking voice went on, "I'm sure he wouldn't want his firm to know that one of their salesmen did a nice little sideline in smuggling. Not just now, particularly, when he wants that new job."

The receiver clicked. The caller had gone, having successfully smeared and ruined her day. For what possible reason, except that he had a grudge against Max, and wanted to ruin his chances of being made export manager?

It must be one of his colleagues. It had to be.

Who? That man O'Brien who had rung

for help the other night?

She had to do something about it. She couldn't sit here meekly being persecuted. Impulsively, with a shaking finger, she dialed the number of Max's firm.

When the girl at the switchboard answered she asked to speak to Mr. O'Brien.

What was she going to say to him? She didn't know. Something would come to her when he answered.

"O'Brien?" repeated the girl. "Just a minute."

The time slid by. Mrs. Ingram peered through the window, watching.

The girl spoke again. "I think you've made a mistake, madam. There's no one here of that name."

"Oh! You mean he's been moved already?"

"No, there was never anyone here called O'Brien."

"Are you new?" Ella asked.

"Certainly I'm not. I've been here two years."

"Oh. Sorry. Then I must have made a mistake."

No O'Brien. So that meant Max had been lying. About how many things besides the fictitious O'Brien's troubles? About Mrs. Gibson, too? Had the mink jacket been for her?

"You all right, Mrs. Simpson?" came Mrs. Ingram's voice.

Ella realized she had been standing clutching the telephone long after it had gone silent.

"Yes. I'm all right. I just had one of those anonymous calls."

"Did he use filthy language?" Mrs. Ingram asked, with indecent eagerness.

"No, he was polite enough. In a queer way."

"You ought to tell the police."

"Oh, I don't think so. It's difficult to trace these calls."

"Brutes," said Mrs. Ingram. "They get their kicks that way. My niece, she was asked if she wore black knickers. Thought it a lark. You ought to laugh about it, Mrs. Simpson. You all of a-tremble like that, that's what they want."

But it's more than an anonymous call, it's things that man with the nasty confidential voice knows about Max and me. The new car, the doctor, Max's job. It must be someone who is insanely jealous of Max. Someone whom Max is a little afraid of.

Because he is in a position to be blackmailed?

Ella had scarcely turned away from the telephone before it rang again. She saw Mrs. Ingram gesticulating through the window, asking if she should come and answer it.

But I won't be a coward, Ella determined, and put out her damp shaky hand.

"Ella?" It was Booth Bramwell's calm voice. She recognized it at once, with pleasure made acute by relief.

"Hullo."

"You sound scared. Something wrong?"

"No. At least — "

"Have you had another of those calls?"

"Yes, I have, as a matter of fact. But it doesn't matter. I'll tell Max."

How could she tell Booth, so new a friend, that someone was accusing Max of smuggling a mink jacket that wasn't even for his wife?

It must have been something to do with

this that had taken Max off on that mysterious errand the evening he had arrived home from abroad. The man O'Brien and his troubles must have been pure invention for her benefit, to stop her suspicions.

Max, how long have you been devious like this without my knowing?

"Ella!"

She jerked herself out of her daydreaming.

"Yes?"

"Is it something you can't tell me?"

"I — don't know."

"Well, I guess we haven't known each other very long, but I have a feeling we could talk. We did yesterday. Come out to lunch."

"Today?"

"Can you suggest a better time?"

"I don't know. Mrs. Ingram's here, and, goodness, it's half past eleven already!"

"How long do you take to get ready? You're not expecting the Ritz or the Savoy, are you? I want to tell you what I found out about the house."

"Oh, yes!" Her voice came alive. She was

astonished that her mood could change so swiftly from fear to eagerness, almost to happiness. There really was some alchemy about that old house. The strong thread of joy that had run through yesterday was coming back.

"Mrs. Ingram! I'll have to leave you to finish the windows without me. I'm going out to lunch."

Mrs. Ingram's eyes, beetle black, glinted.

"Well, I never. That wasn't your anonymous caller saying something nice for a change?"

Ella didn't believe in relating all her affairs to a domestic help, but since Booth would shortly be at the door there was no point in being anything but frank.

"It's Mr. Bramwell next door," she said casually. "We have some things to discuss. Tell my husband if he rings."

And don't get that insinuating note in your voice. A walk with Mr. Bramwell yesterday, lunch today. Never mind, it won't do Max any harm the way he's been treating me lately. And he has some explaining to do himself. . . .

Talking to yourself again, Ella chided. It

was a sure sign of mental deterioration. Or just euphoria. But wasn't that a sign of mental trouble, also, a too-sudden swing from depression to euphoria?

And if I were a bit mad, I couldn't analyze that about myself, could I?

Booth knew a restaurant where they could sit outdoors. It was the only thing to do on a day like this. And suddenly Ella was reveling in the heat. It was deliciously relaxing, making her shed her inhibitions. She had put on her dark-blue linen dress, low-cut and sleeveless, and tied her hair back with one of Kitty's red ribbons. She was no longer weary and washed-out, but part of the beautiful warm blurred radiance that lay over the country like a benediction.

Since the restaurant was a mile or so away she suggested they go in the car, and then, if Booth could spare the time, they could pick Kitty up on their way home.

"Splendid," he said. "If Kitty doesn't mind."

"Kitty sees no one but Sam. So don't think you're going to make a big hit with her. Tell me about the house."

"Patience. Wait until lunch."

Nobody followed Max's smart new car today. Or perhaps she was too conscious of her passenger to notice. It was apprehension and loneliness that made one imagine things. She was prepared to believe now that she had never been followed or watched or spoken to by a strange man with obscuring dark glasses.

Their table was the farthest from the restaurant, the nearest to the slow-flowing dark-green river. Ella surreptitiously kicked off her shoes and felt the cool grass beneath her feet.

"I love it," she said. "It's like one of those delicious green swoony paintings at Royal Academy exhibitions. 'River with Swans.' Why have Max and I never found this place? But then we don't eat out very much. With a young child, one doesn't. Well, one either has children or one has nights out."

"I'm glad you like it," said Booth noncommittally.

"So that's two nice things. The old house and garden yesterday, and here today. Everything isn't horrid."

"Are other things?"

"Sort of."

"That telephone call?"

"Don't let's talk about it now. I want to know about the house."

Booth signaled to a waiter. Without consulting Ella he ordered chilled consomme, lobster salad, and a bottle of white wine. "All right?" he asked her.

"Absolutely right."

"Good. And two large dry martinis to begin," he added.

"Hey, I'm driving Max's new car!"

"Why Max's new car? Why not yours?"

"Oh, well. That's the way I see it. I wanted a baby, and Max wanted a new car. A status symbol. It's a pity babies can't be status symbols. But they can't, can they? They're too easy. They don't represent achievement, cleverness, drive and ambition. Any old fool can have them. Stop me, Booth. Lately I've developed this habit of thinking aloud. Mrs. Ingram thinks I'm around the bend. So does Max, sometimes."

"Talk as much as you like."

"But why to you? I ought to be terrified of you. At least, Max thinks I should."

"And why should someone like you be

188

terrified of someone like me?"

"Well. . . . Scatty Ella."

Booth said quietly, "I think you have an original and refreshing mind."

"Oh. Thank you, Mr. Brontë."

"For God's sake, don't be humble! It doesn't suit you."

"I'm not usually." Now she found she was humbly apologizing. "It's just that I've felt a bit stupid and dumb lately. I don't know why."

"Here's your drink."

"And I need it. Don't say it for me." She sipped the ice-cold drink, and leaned forward eagerly. "Now forget me and talk about the house."

He gave the slow smile she liked. It lightened his serious face.

"Well, I'll tell you all I did find out. I searched the title, and then went to the family's solicitor."

"Did you really? How clever of you to track them down."

"Deviling, they call it. I pretended I was interested in buying the house. So the senior member of the firm, a very old chap who was allowed to remain in the office out of courtesy, I should think, was delighted to tell me the family's history. The last owner was an old woman who died there. Miss Edith Grimshaw."

"Edith!"

"A granddaughter of your Edith whose father, Joseph Knott, built the house in 1842. He was a pretty well-heeled early Victorian with a jeweler's business in Holborn. I gather he had a town house, and this was to be his country house. He intended to retire to it when he gave up business."

"And Edith wore his diamonds."

"Stop romanticizing. I'm telling you facts."

"Go on," Ella begged.

"Joseph Knott had seven children."

"But that's what I told Kitty! You see, I do have this fey thing about that house."

"Then you're not going to like what comes next. Edith was the eldest daughter and her father's favorite child. But when she was eighteen she eloped with her music teacher — "

"How marvelous! And then she was cut off by her father."

"So you know that, too."

"But of course she would be. Those times, those sort of parents."

"Absolutely right. In those times, the sons in a family inherited, anyway. But later, it seems, the father did relent and while he left his business to his sons, and legacies to his other children, he decided to forgive Edith and left her the country house."

"I'm so glad."

"So she lived there until she died in 1899, and then the place went to her only son, Ernest Grimshaw, and he left it to his only daughter, Edith, who never married. She died there, an eccentric old spinster, in 1960. She was ninety-one, and she had practically no money, so the place had been allowed to go to pieces. It was left to a distant cousin in Canada who never did anything about it, except claim compensation when the council took it over recently for a road-widening scheme. It's to be demolished in the near future. So there you are, there's nothing very out of the ordinary about all that."

"I suppose not. Only Edith eloping. I like

that. I wonder why I got so obsessed by that house."

"Simply because it reminded you of the house you lived in as a child."

"You mean I was subconsciously trying to escape back into childhood."

"Perhaps."

Ella frowned. "What's the significance of that?"

"Well, it usually means some discontent with the present."

"My marriage isn't unhappy."

"I didn't say that."

The food had arrived, and Ella ate, hoping to escape from a suddenly flat feeling. There it was again, this swoop from euphoria to uncertainty and depression.

"It's only since Sunday, since Max got back from the continent and has been in a difficult mood," she said defensively. "He has a lot on his mind."

"Didn't you have this pleasure in the old house before Max got back?"

"Yes," Ella admitted reluctantly. "That's true. So you think I wasn't happy, even then?"

"Who knows what's in a subconscious?"

192

"You think I hate the house we're living in? Well, that's true, I do. And I long for a lovely wild garden. But that isn't hating my husband."

"Of course not."

"And I have been aggravating to Max with my awful absentmindedness. He has such a tidy mind. All the same — "

"All the same, what?"

Booth's interest was absolutely sincere, she thought. Her rather excessive gratitude to him for that must represent another form of insecurity.

"I don't think he's been telling me the truth," she said slowly.

"Do you want to talk to me about it?"

She prevaricated.

"I'll certainly have to talk to Max."

"The telephone calls are about this?"

"I think someone's blackmailing him, through me. Using my gullibility, perhaps."

She was grateful again for his concerned look. The temptation to tell Booth everything was growing stronger than her loyalty to Max.

"This man this morning said something about a mink jacket that Max was supposed to have smuggled through customs." She paused, and lifted wounded eyes. "The jacket wasn't for me."

"So you'll have to talk to him about it."

"Yes. He won't like it."

"Naturally."

"I can't really believe it's true. Max is too sensible to risk doing such a crazy thing."

"But you'll have to find out."

"He'll say I imagined that call. He'll say it's all in my subconscious because I want to hurt him. Just as you say I loved that old house because I want to escape into childhood again."

"Mrs. Simpson, darling," said Booth.

Ella looked at his hand laid over hers. He had this capacity for tenderness, she thought. How could his wife have left him, when he possessed a gift so valuable to women?

Yet he didn't look a tender person. Which made its sudden display all the more endearing.

"Anyway, didn't Mrs. Ingram hear the call?"

"Yes, but she didn't hear what the man said. It might have been about the laundry as far as she was concerned."

"One doesn't send mink coats to a laundry."

Ella began to laugh. "Booth, for an egghead, you're rather idiotic — " She stopped, her eyes widening.

"What's the matter?"

"That man over there. At that table by the veranda. With dark glasses."

Booth turned casually to look.

"What about him?"

"He has that sort of smoke-colored face. I'm sure he's the man who followed me in the car on Monday, and stopped to talk to me yesterday. I'm sure he's the one who's following me."

"Ella, who could be following you?"

"That's what I want to know," she said, her voice rising.

She clenched her hands. Now keep calm, keep calm, otherwise Booth, this nice wise man, will be telling you you're gaga, too.

"Do you think he's the person who's ringing you?"

"How do I know?"

"You said he spoke to you yesterday in the car."

"Yes, he did. But his voice sounded quite ordinary. Voices sound different on the telephone. More so, if you know what I mean."

"I do. And they can be exaggerated if the caller's a bit of an actor."

Ella put down her napkin. Panic was flowing over her in an irresistible tide. "Booth, let's go."

He put a delaying hand on her arm.

"Why are you running away? Besides, I haven't paid the bill."

"I'll go to the ladies' room while you do."

"Ella! No one can hurt you!"

"I can't bear him staring at me through those horrible black glasses!" Compulsively, she shot up and was hurrying across the lawn between the tables, almost running.

Idiot! Coward! she told her image in the mirror. But not for several minutes, not until she had splashed her face with cold water and got her breath back.

Why did you have to run away? Now Booth, too, will think your sanity leaves a lot to be desired. He's good on diagnosis.

He'll be on to that persecution complex in a flash.

But the man *was* there, sitting watching her. She couldn't even go out to lunch in peace.

Her enormous eyes, scared and overbright, were like Kitty's when she woke from a nightmare. She hastily put on lipstick, smoothed her hair, tried to look normal.

When she came out Booth was waiting in the foyer, and outside, on the square of green lawn bathed in the hot hazy sunlight, the table where the man with the smoke-colored face had sat was empty.

"He left just before I did," Booth said, reading her thoughts. "I'd lost him by the time I got out here. I rather think he drove off in a green Mini."

"It was a green Mini outside our house yesterday," Ella said breathlessly. "Just sitting there. I thought the two men in it were watching our house, but Max said that was nonsense, they couldn't have been interested in us, otherwise why didn't they ring the doorbell?"

"You didn't tell me about this."

"No, because you'd have thought I was crazy and laughed at me, too. Wouldn't you?"

"I wouldn't have laughed. I wouldn't have thought you crazy either. Just overimaginative perhaps. A car stopped on the other side of the street — "

"And those men with narrow faces."

"A type in your mind?" Booth suggested. "Too much television?"

"Like Sam with his gun!" Ella exclaimed indignantly.

"Nothing wrong with that. After all, we were both a little imaginative about the old house yesterday, and I assume this happened just after we got back."

"Yes, it did."

"But the men didn't stay long, sitting in the car?"

"No. Max rang, and when I looked out again, they'd gone."

"Well, there you are. Anyway, there are thousands of green Minis. It would be a long chance that the one I just saw was the same one."

His voice was gentle and calming. It made Ella's skin prickle with frustration.

"I *know* one can rationalize," she said. "But this whole thing isn't rational. It simply isn't."

Chapter 10

"I don't know how to say this," Booth said later, as they sat in the car waiting for Kitty to come out of school, "but has it occurred to you that your husband might be playing a trick on you?"

"How?"

"Faking those telephone calls."

"You mean disguising his voice, pretending to be a stranger!" Ella's voice rose high with incredulity. "But why should he do a horrible thing like that?"

Booth shrugged.

"If he's been bringing home expensive presents for another woman."

"And he wants me to know, so he gives me a hint in this kinky way."

"A bit farfetched, I expect," Booth murmured apologetically.

"It is. For one thing, Max is no actor. I don't believe he could change his voice like that."

"It isn't difficult, on a telephone, when you can't see the caller's face. Some heavy breathing, voice lowered or whispering. You don't need to do much to get a sinister effect."

"You sound an expert on it!" Ella cried angrily. "In a minute I'll be accusing you."

He laughed. "Now why on earth would I do something like that?"

"I don't know. For kicks. Like Mrs. Ingram says."

"You ought to be ashamed of yourself, Mrs. Simpson."

She was ashamed. She said quickly, "I'm only saying that it's as impossible for you to do that as it is for Max. Neither of you — well, it would just be impossible. So we're back to the sinister stranger. The man with the dark glasses."

"Then can you think why he would be doing it? Apart from kicks?"

"I haven't the slightest idea. Unless he's a professional sadist. But, Booth" — the sun was so hot, coming in the window of the car, it made her feel intensely weary — "Max loves me. He always has, and I've done nothing to make him stop in the last few days, except irritate him with my absentmindedness. But that isn't grounds for a divorce." She stopped for a moment, following a now uneasy thought. "It couldn't be that he wants me to divorce him?"

"Only if he's quite mad."

"Thank you, Booth," she said gratefully. "Do you forgive me for what I said?"

"What did you say, my darling?"

"So ridiculous. That there was any likelihood of you being my persecutor on the telephone."

"You and Kitty," Booth said roughly, "you'll both have to grow thicker skins. Though I like this one." His fingers moved tentatively on her bare arm, then he took them away, looking angry with himself.

Ella didn't let herself dwell on that contact which she had liked. She reverted to their original discussion.

"Besides, Max thinks I'll be the right sort of wife for this new job he's hoping to get."

"Good God, you're not married to a job!"

"One is, more or less. If it's a good marriage. If one identifies completely with one's husband. And isn't a maddened follower of women's liberation." Her lips quirked. "If there is this other woman, she wouldn't be the right kind. I mean, accepting mink jackets from a married man. Max wouldn't approve of that sort of behavior from someone who was to be his wife. I know. I know him absolutely."

"Do you?"

"You can't live and sleep with someone for six years without knowing them like another part of yourself."

"That's only true of sensitive women. Not — " He was going to say not his wife, but didn't.

Ella covered his hesitation by saying, "Not Mrs. Daphne Gibson, for instance."

"Now, why do you bring her into it?"

Ella squirmed beneath his too-inquisitive gaze. She was Kitty found out in a vague untruth which she couldn't explain. Mrs. Daphne Gibson had floated into her mind, out of the blue, and now those keen eyes were judging her and finding her wanting in adult intelligence.

"I honestly don't know. I've had this stupid feeling that Max knows that woman. He was furious when I asked him. Too furious. I wondered why afterward." Her voice trailed away.

When Booth didn't speak she demanded in agony, "You don't think I'm a little odd, do you? Queer, neurotic, gaga? Max thinks I have a persecution complex," she added miserably.

"You're certainly under some stress," Booth said, after considering. "Why is that?"

"*Why!* Because of those telephone calls, those men watching, always someone following me, bumping my car, giving me dire warnings! Wouldn't you be under stress in those circumstances?"

"I suppose I would be."

"But you don't believe the circumstances exist!"

"Well, all I've seen with my own eyes is a stranger wearing dark glasses eating in a restaurant. And your fear," he added, after a moment.

"Do I seem so frightened?" Ella was ashamed of her cowardice.

"Frightened to death."

She put her hands to her face, whispering, "Am I?"

"And that's either because these things are happening, someone is trying to scare you to death, or because one shock — such as the police calling, for instance — has sparked off a chain of latent fears in your subconscious." He raised his eyebrows, and stopped looking serious. "That's jargon even I don't understand. You'd have to get a doctor to sort that out."

She leaned toward him, clutching his hands.

"Now you're talking of doctors! What do you really think of me?"

"Why, that you're a charming innocent little dreamer." He bent and dropped quick soft kisses on her forehead and her cheeks, saying between them, "Like Kitty — neither of you tough enough — should keep away from rough males."

Ella sat quite still, her face uplifted like a flower catching raindrops after a parched day. That happiness, much too elusive to last, was with her again.

"Max says you're an egghead," she murmured.

Booth stopped kissing her.

"So you talked about me?"

"Of course. I told him about your sister offering to babysit and he said we might go out one night." She didn't tell him about the evening to be spent with four jolly German businessmen.

"Ella."

"What?"

"Whatever I've said, and I'm guessing as much as you are, you're going to get to the bottom of this mink jacket business, aren't you?"

Ella's happiness vanished at once, but a strong streak of anger replaced it, making her say grimly, "You can be sure. You can be very sure."

Ella could hear the telephone ringing, with its high-pitched burr, like a demented canary, before she had stopped the car in the driveway.

Booth said, "Like me to answer it?"

Kitty and Sam had hurtled out of the car and made for the back garden. Ella, fumbling with shaking fingers for the door key, shook her head vehemently. Could she allow herself to be even more of a coward than she already was?

"No. I must. But wait a minute, if you don't mind. I expect it will stop before I get there anyway." Her voice was so breathless that she also doubted if she would be able to speak audibly.

However, the caller was only Max, and when he heard her voice he sounded as if he shared her relief.

"Ella, where on earth have you been? I've been ringing ever since lunch."

"Getting Kitty."

"Not since two o'clock!"

"Oh, I did some shopping." She had suddenly made the decision not to tell him about her lunch with Booth Bramwell. It only made another complication.

"For two hours! In this heat!"

"Actually I wanted to stay out of the house."

His voice came sharply. "Why? Has

207

something happened?"

As if he expected something to have happened. . . .

"Yes. In a way. I can't tell you about it on the telephone. Be home early, Max, please."

"Is it the police?"

"No. They've left me strictly alone today."

"Not that crazy idea that someone's watching you?"

"*No,* Max. Just come home, will you, please?"

"Okay, okay. I'll be there as soon as I can. Look, if you're scared don't answer the telephone."

How did he know that it was another threatening telephone call that had happened? She hadn't said so.

How did he know, unless he had made it himself . . . ?

"It's all right, Booth," she said, coming outside. "It was only Max. He'll be home soon."

"Good. Then I'll go. I ought to be in Fleet Street by six, and the time the trains take nowadays — "

She loved him suddenly, standing there in his crumpled shirt and baggy trousers, his face kind and frankly anxious. She wanted badly to beg him to stay, at least until his sister Lorna got home, so that she knew she had someone within call. The people who lived in the house on the other side were away on a month's holiday, and she couldn't go rushing across the street to virtual strangers.

But she was used to being here alone with Kitty in the mellowing afternoon, alone all night, too, when Max was traveling.

A few strange telephone calls, a speeding gray Jaguar that she hadn't even seen, shouldn't make her feel so totally alone and vulnerable.

"If the telephone rings again, don't answer it."

"That's what Max said."

"Then do that, eh?" He gave his slightly bashful tender smile and went away rather slowly, rather heavily, as if he were weighed down with anxieties and ruminations.

But how could he be, since he didn't really take her fears seriously? He humored her because he quite admired her.

But he didn't think it was an act of cruelty to leave her alone.

She sat on the terrace and watched Kitty and Sam splashing in the scarlet rubber pool. Sam, that freckle-faced little tough guy, had a streak of tenderness, too, for he sprang out of the water to carefully move the shabby perambulator out of harm's way.

"You shouldn't leave them in the boiling sun," he told Kitty.

"Thank you, Sam. You are kind."

"Their faces might melt."

"Especially Edith's. She's used to a parasol."

Perhaps after all Kitty had better marry Sam when she grew up, since he could enter into her dream. That was a more important asset to have in a husband than she had realized. Sam and Mr. Brontë. Gauche shy tender people.

Max wasn't any of those things. Max, sharp and well dressed, was standing over her, saying in his quick impatient way, "Well, what was it you couldn't tell me over the telephone?"

She knew by his tone that he wasn't in a

mood to believe her. He had believed her when she had spoken on the telephone. But since then he had had time to compose himself, to prepare his attitude. She was almost certain of that, so she decided she would make no attempt to cushion this particular piece of information. She was getting cunning. She wanted to watch his first unguarded reaction.

"I had another of those funny telephone calls today."

"Oh, lord!" He assumed a look of boredom. She knew he wasn't in the least bored.

"It was the same man. He said did I know you had smuggled a mink coat through customs."

"Not a mink!" The words burst out before he could control them. And there it was again in his so well-known face, the flash of panic, before it was rapidly replaced by astonishment and indignation. Ella found herself admiring his remarkable self-control. This was what had made him so successful in business negotiations, of course.

But if it hadn't been a mink, had it been

something else? For the instantaneous guilt had been there, the panic, the look of fear. The knowledge filled Ella with misery.

"Me smuggling mink coats!" he went on in high indignation. "You didn't believe that?"

"It wasn't mink coats, it was a mink jacket. In the singular."

"And I'm supposed to have brought it in without paying duty. But you unpacked for me, you know it wasn't in my luggage."

"Does that necessarily prove anything?"

"Ella! Are you suggesting I might have dropped it off to a girlfriend on the way home? My God, are you really suggesting that?"

His eyes were hard, his face tight with fury. But was he a little too vehement, as he had been when he had denied knowing Mrs. Daphne Gibson?

Ella was ashamed of her suspicion, and unable to get rid of it.

"I don't know. What am I supposed to believe when I'm told a thing like that?"

Max stood over her, too close, making her feel crushed and claustrophobic.

"Are you sure this happened? Positive?

You know you've been doing funny things lately."

"Now don't say my uncertain mental state could invent that."

"I honestly don't know what it could invent. I can only assure you that this particular thing isn't true. Good heavens, Ella, you know me."

She did. She was almost certain he had never looked seriously at another woman since they had been married. Not because he was so passionately in love with her, but because he was too ambitious, and apart from affairs being too risky, he needed all his time and energy to pursue his career. There was nothing wrong with his sexual ability, but lately Ella had begun to suspect that he was cold emotionally. Take his attitude toward the loss of the new baby. It had been one of relief, although he had tried to disguise the fact.

No, if he had a woman hidden away it would be a passing affair. One which he probably already regretted. Was the mink jacket intended to be a farewell gift? If there had been a mink jacket. . . .

"Then why should someone ring me up to

tell me that?" she asked.

"Search me. If it happened."

"Max, would I be in this state if I were making this up? Why should I make such a thing up?" she added helplessly.

"Then it must be someone who's jealous of me, wants to ruin my chances with the firm."

"O'Brien?" Ella murmured.

"Perhaps."

"If there is actually anyone called O'Brien."

Again the alarm, quickly veiled, leaped in his eyes.

"Now you're suggesting I'm inventing things."

"Which is only what you've been doing to me."

"Oh, Ella love!" For a moment he was bewildered, contrite, the old Max whom now, with his growing success and confidence, she hardly ever saw.

"If it's a telephone maniac, we ought to tell the police," she urged. "Booth thinks so."

"Booth?"

"Mr. Brontë."

"God, you haven't been telling him!"

Her chin went up. "Why not? I have to talk to someone or go mad — I mean, not mad, but — "

"You are mad," Max interrupted coldly. "Blabbing our private affairs to a stranger. What else have you told him?"

"Only about the old house. He found out who it belonged to because he knew I was so interested."

"Ella, you haven't been there again?"

"Yes, why not? Booth came with me." She decided she might as well be hanged for a sheep as a lamb.

"When I especially asked you not to," Max said angrily.

"You only asked me not to mention it to the police. I don't know why you did that."

"Because you've somehow gone gaga about that filthy old place. You're like a little girl playing houses. I can't stand it. My wife, a grown woman — "

The telephone ringing cut off his distracted protest. He jumped, as if he had become as nervous as Ella was, then strode off to answer it, again banging the living-room door behind him.

Ella stayed where she was, too tired to listen at keyholes, not wanting any more shocks.

However, the caller had chosen a bad moment, when Max's temper was inflammable, for presently his voice rose and was clearly audible.

"I tell you it wasn't with my knowledge. I was in my office all day, as you very well know. . . . Look here, if you don't stop interfering in my life. No, they haven't. . . . And can I ask you what went wrong at your end? I suppose you were too clumsy. . . . No, *you* be careful. In the end I might pack the whole thing in . . . ."

But he wouldn't. If it were the new job he was talking about. It was his unalterable goal, his Everest.

"Someone from the office?" Ella asked, when he came back into the living room and made for the drinks cabinet, keeping his face turned away from her.

"That's right."

"I heard you say you might pack it in. The job?"

"Yes, I might."

"Oh, Max." She went to put her arm

216

around him. "Who *is* this who rings you up worrying you?"

He splashed whiskey into a glass.

"I told you. A rival. One of my own salesmen," he added belatedly.

"Threatening you! Why don't you sack him?"

"He wasn't threatening me, he was only telling me about something that went wrong. It'll be put right tomorrow and then" — Max sighed deeply as if he were terribly tired — "we can relax. That'll be nice, won't it?"

"Yes, it will, but — "

"But what?"

"Never mind." It would be unwise to say she had this feeling that Max's caller each evening was her caller of the mornings. The man with the husky jeering voice. There was a significant pattern about the calls. Moreover, it was extremely hard to believe that Max would be so agitated by a call from one of his salesmen. Not O'Brien, he was canny enough not to mention a name this time.

"All the same, I wish I knew what was going on. I don't think I can put up with this mystery much longer."

"No mystery, love, except what your lurid imagination invents." Max ruffled her hair with a heavy hand. She guessed it was meant to be affectionate. "There's a bit of mud slinging going on, that's all. You have to expect it when there's a lot at stake. But if we can get through tomorrow, and possibly the next day, and you behave yourself and look after Kitty, all will be well, I promise you."

Ella was not reassured.

"Now you're being just as mysterious yourself. It's as if you're suggesting Kitty or I might be in danger."

"Any pretty blonds, like my wife and daughter, can be in danger, given the right circumstances. In these wicked times."

Ella looked startled, then laughed.

"Honestly, and you accuse me of being melodramatic. Do you really think Kitty and I might be kidnapped like Mrs. Daphne Gibson?"

He did! She saw it in his face.

But at once he was saying lightly, "Of course not. But stay at home. Stop wandering. Stop talking to your ridiculous

Mr. Brontë. If that's where you're getting your theatrical ideas."

"Oh, no, he's very calm, very sensible."

"But he's encouraged you about that damned creepy house. So give them, he and the house both, a wide berth."

Ella's mind, even if it were diverted down different avenues of thought, kept coming back to the same point.

"Then was the mink jacket part of the mud slinging?"

"Of course it was."

"It's his word against yours?"

"His?"

"This rival."

"I suppose so. He's got no proof, but a smear like that — "

"It's wicked."

"I know, but forget it now." Max seemed anxious to forget it himself, if not to dismiss it as more of her fantasy. "What are we having for supper?"

"Oh, my God!"

"Now what?"

"I forgot to shop. I was going to buy smoked salmon and brown bread and strawberries. But what with going out to lunch and waiting for Kitty — all the same, how could I have forgotten?"

Max's eyebrows were raised, his gaze had become uncharacteristically patient and tolerant, almost pleased. That was the most upsetting thing of all. He was glad she had been so forgetful. It proved what he had been saying for the last three days. Her mind was in a most peculiar state. . . .

"Never mind, love, we'll have what there is. And you make an appointment to see Doctor Greave as soon as you can. I want a functioning wife, not a zombie. Wandering in the fields, stripping my garden, forgetting to shop, imagining she's being followed by strange men. You've got to get over this, Ella. You've got to get well."

That litany, thank goodness, was brought to an end by Kitty and Sam appearing in the doorway. Scantily clad, her long hair streaky with water, Kitty looked like a mermaid, Sam something much more robust.

"Can we watch television? Sam wants to," Kitty said.

"It's late, isn't Sam's mother expecting him?" Ella asked. She didn't think Max was in any mood for two children goggle-eyed over a Western (it would have to be a Western since inevitably it would be Sam's choice), but unexpectedly Max retained his previous tolerance. He switched on the set for them and inadvertently caught the tail end of the news.

It was something about Mrs. Gibson's kidnapping. *"The police refused to comment on the rumor that a ransom demand for twenty thousand pounds had, in fact, been made, and was thought to be genuine. Earlier, Mr. Gibson made an appeal to the men believed to be holding his wife to return her safely, for the sake of her children."*

The picture flashed from the bland face of the announcer to that of the pugnacious heavy-browed industrialist, Mr. Gibson, then to two fair-haired little girls. Blonds, Ella thought involuntarily. Mrs. Daphne Gibson had been — *was* — a blond, too, according to her picture.

Abruptly Max switched the set to another channel. He was scowling again. "Not fit for kids," he muttered. "You never know what you'll see inside this damn box."

"I think after all Sam had better go home," said Ella nervously. "It's getting dark."

"It's not, it's light as day, Mrs. Simpson," Sam protested.

"Why, Mummy? Do you think the kidnappers might be about?" Kitty asked, her eyes too wide.

"Of course they won't be," Max said irritably. "But do as you're told, Sam. Run along home."

Sam hung his lower lip, but didn't dare dispute with Kitty's father, for whom he had a healthy respect.

"Then we'd better get the family in," he muttered to Kitty.

"Oh, yes. Before it's dark."

They scampered out, and Ella murmured, "He is rather sweet, the way he's so patient with Kitty and her foibles."

"So am I patient with you."

"Sometimes."

"All the time. More than you know."

Because she had done other odd things, the knowledge of which he had kindly spared her? Ella determined not to brood. Who was she to be sorry for herself, when there was that desperately worried Mr. Gibson and the two little girls?

She said brightly, "Max, do you realize you haven't had the new car out? I thought you wouldn't be able to wait to try it."

"H'mm? I'm too tired. We'll go for a run at the weekend. Get some fresh air. Relax."

"Your worries will be over by the weekend?"

"Sure." He gave a half grin, the old Max again, briefly. "Except for you, my nutty little wife, of course."

But that small cruelty was at least spoken with affection.

Nevertheless, she slept badly again (as she knew Max did, too), and was wide awake at five o'clock. Unable to lie any longer in the bed that was so hot even though their bodies were not touching, she got up quietly and went on the landing to draw back the curtains and look at the warm still dawn.

The sky was shell pink, ineffably serene, with its low crocheted border of hedges and rooftops and chimneys. In the clear early morning air the trees around the old house and some of its chimneys were much more sharply visible than they would be later when the heat haze had muffled them.

A plume of smoke from one of the chimneys hung like a gray feather across the pink dawn.

Smoke! Who had lighted a fire in the ballroom of the empty house?

She knew it was the ballroom. She could see it, the yellow flames licking up the chimney, just as she had so positively seen Edith in her ball gown.

You're dreaming again, Ella. That's forbidden.

But who had lighted the fire? With rising excitement, and a twinge of fear, Ella knew that this was a mystery she would not be able to leave unsolved. No matter what stern orders Max had given her. . . .

Chapter 11

Thursday morning. The week was nearly over, without a break in the heat wave. The golden-guinea sun was already high in the sky, it was going to be another day with soaring temperatures.

Max told Ella to go into the West End and buy the new dress he wanted her to have for the dinner party.

"It'll do you good to get out of the house," he said.

To get away from the telephone was what he meant.

"Get something exciting, glamorous. I want you to be the best-dressed woman there."

As an extension of himself, of course. How much was genuine pride in her and how much his own vanity? Ella was shocked

225

at herself. Never previously had she asked such questions as this.

"I don't think I feel in the mood," she said.

The quick nervy impatience twitched in his face, then was hastily smoothed away.

"I call that a bit ungrateful. Sulking because you're told to buy an expensive dress."

"I'm not sulking. But can you imagine trying on clothes on a day like this? I'll make a mistake and buy something quite wrong."

"Love, you couldn't do that if you tried. You've got good taste."

Ella shrugged. She felt mean. She knew how hard he was trying for normality, but he couldn't see his face across the breakfast table, sallow and tired and ten years older than it had been a week ago.

If this was the price of becoming export manager, what would it cost to be managing director? Would they have to go through this curious torture again and again, during Max's compulsive climb up the ladder of success?

All the same, even Ella's woolly mind

could not be convinced that there wasn't something more sinister than competitiveness over a new job going on. Somehow, they had acquired a bitter enemy.

It was useless to go on asking questions merely to get evasive answers. Very well, she would follow Max's suggestion and have an active, well-filled day. First, take Kitty to school, then make that short detour she had secretly planned before she returned home to change for her trip to London. Later, back in time to collect Kitty, and to invite Booth over for iced tea if he could spare the time.

He had already spared her too much of his time, therefore she wouldn't ask him to accompany her on this swift imperative visit to the old house. After dropping Kitty she would drive on until she found the front gates where the NO TRESPASSING sign hung. Then she would boldly take the car up the front drive, and find out whether the fire still burned on Edith's hearth.

She could not have explained to anyone at all, not even Booth, why she had this overwhelming compulsion to see that all was well at the old house.

The screech owl, the closed window, and now the smoke from the chimney. In some strange way, these things must add up. To what?

You have an obsessive form of madness, Mrs. Simpson. You allow yourself to be possessed by the dream of a house you would like to have lived in. Your husband says you also have hallucinations, you hear voices, like Joan of Arc did, only through the modern medium of the telephone, you see things that don't exist, such as men in dark glasses watching you, such as smoke from dead chimneys. . . .

But the smoke hadn't been an hallucination. Ella gave a small cry of triumph when she let herself into the ballroom, opening the French windows by putting her hand through the broken pane of glass. The ashes had been swept away, but small deposits of soot, no doubt loosened by the heat, had fallen down the chimney, and the bricks of the hearth were still warm to her touch. The room quite definitely smelled of smoke.

Ella was amazed at her temerity. She had

driven up the curving drive flanked by the dismal laurel bushes, left the car at the front door, and hastened around to the garden, the sweet-smelling sunny refuge that she loved. There was no one about.

There could, of course, be someone somewhere in the house, but she was sure there was not. It was too quiet, with a palpable atmosphere of peace. Nevertheless, someone had been there and had lighted a fire to prove it.

Now why, on such a warm night, would a tramp have lighted a fire? To cook by? And then, on departure, to neatly sweep up the ashes and remove all, or almost all, signs of his illegal occupation. Perhaps he had been a hippie with memories of a house-proud mother and an indelible childhood training to be neat and tidy.

But why had he wanted his fire so early in the morning?

Because no one would be about, of course.

Though would it matter so much if he had been caught dossing down in a house scheduled for demolition?

Whoever he was, he had gone now. The

stillness was complete. It must have been as still as this when ancient Miss Grimshaw, the last Edith, lay dead. For it was the quietness of death, Ella fancied, and suddenly melancholy came over her. She stepped out onto the terrace, shutting the door behind her, as tidy as the previous intruder had been.

The garden was deep in its drowsy peace, the white butterflies blown light as bubbles in the air, the bees humming, the wind sighing in the trees. The air was hot and heavy. Above the scent of wallflowers Ella thought she could still smell smoke. It seemed, too, that some of the long grass was flattened. A slightly bruised swathe led crookedly across the garden to the dark untidy jungle of overgrown privet and rhododendron. The path of a badger or a fox?

A tree rustled. Something moved. A squirrel? A wood pigeon?

It was a Sleeping Beauty garden, with its sunny tranquillity disguising thorns, and vague menace.

The thorns were real enough, but the menace was only in her mind.

Ella shook herself physically, knowing she must also shake her mind free of this strange obsession. She was transferring her suspicions and insecurity to inanimate objects. She must become entirely practical. No more dreaming.

Home now, and nothing said about the self-indulgence of this visit, even to Booth.

She drove away fast down the drive and edged onto the busy highway. A green Mini shot past her, traveling at high speed. She couldn't see the driver's face.

There were dozens of cars on the road. At least ten percent of them would be Minis, green, red, whatever.

She made her fingers on the wheel unclench. Hadn't she determined to get rid of this trauma?

The house was as she had left it, breakfast dishes on the table, beds unmade, the flowers in the living room, poor Max's plundered garden, beginning to wither and smell bad. She shouldn't have picked them. She might have known cut flowers wouldn't last in his heat.

The house was so dreary at this hour, it was the time she hated, with Max and Kitty gone, Mrs. Ingram not arrived, and all this clutter about. Clear it up today and tomorrow it would be the same. An unending succession of half-empty coffee cups, dirty porridge bowls, plates sticky with marmalade.

Even when Max got his new job and they moved to a bigger house it would be the same, ad infinitum.

There was Kitty's dolls' pram on the patio, carefully in the shade. It was a wonder Kitty didn't insist on taking it to school. She would have been entranced with the new baby. She would have completely entered its world. The three of them, Ella, Kitty, the new baby. . . . There she was, dreaming again. And she could hear Mrs. Ingram at the back door.

She quickly arranged a bright expression in keeping with her planned busy day.

"Good morning, Mrs. Ingram. I'm so glad you're early because I'm going to town. My husband wants me to buy a new dress for a party."

"That's nice, Mrs. Simpson," said Mrs. Ingram, her black eyes giving their moist gleam. "He spoils you, don't he?"

"Well, perhaps. Now and then."

He wants me to be a credit to him, but then so do I want him to be a credit to me. Look at when I take him home, and Daddy gives him that look saying "Slick city gentleman." Well, that's who I married of my own free will, a slick city gentleman.

"Hot again, ain't it?" Mrs. Ingram took off her mackintosh and hung it up. "Killing, really. Anything special you want me to do today, Mrs. Simpson?"

"No, just tidy up. Don't do too much. It really is too hot. I'll take the car to the station and go up by train. If anyone rings — "

Now why had she said that, for her thought communicated itself to the telephone which at that precise moment began its high-pitched ringing.

"Shall I answer it, Mrs. Simpson? You look sort of scared."

No, I'm not, I'm determined to get over this trauma. If that is that horrible man I'll tell him what I think of him.

But the familiar voice dispensed with preliminaries this morning. It said merely, "Where's Kitty?" and the telephone clicked

233

before she could get a word out.

"What is it? A wrong number?" asked Mrs. Ingram. The smell of hot coffee came from the kitchen. Mrs. Ingram was preparing for her usual ritual of a sit and a chat. "Did you see that Mr. Gibson on the telly last night? Looked as if he'd been a bit of a lad in his day. But I was sorry for them poor kids, I don't care what their parents is. Shocking for them, their Mum disappeared like that."

Where's Kitty? . . .

"She won't be found alive, I say, even if the kidnappers get their ransom money. It was to be left in a telephone box in one of them lonely lanes, I heard. But they didn't collect because two lovers disturbed them. Fancy, what a lark!"

Had the sinister caller just rung from a telephone box in a lonely lane?

Where's Kitty?

"Mind you, that's only hearsay. Where you off to, Mrs. Simpson?"

"Just out for ten minutes." Ella was searching frantically for her car keys. "An errand," she mumbled, and banged the door behind her.

The long corridor of the school echoed to her hurrying footsteps. She collided with someone around a corner.

"The infant room?" she asked breathlessly. "Is it this way?"

"Turn left at the end. First door."

First door. Here it was. And a cheerful babble of voices that fell into an abrupt silence as she burst in.

The girl on the rostrum, slim and fair-haired, looking not much older than her charges, raised her eyebrows inquiringly.

"Kitty?" Ella gasped. "My daughter, Kitty Simpson."

"Kitty! Stand up, dear. Is it something important, Mrs. Simpson? Do you want to take her outside?"

Kitty left her desk and came forward in her composed way, her large eyes only faintly inquiring.

"What's the matter, Mummy?"

There seemed to be several hundred pairs of eyes staring at her. Including those of the young schoolmistress.

They all think you're mad, Ella. Rushing in here like that when your daughter's perfectly all right, as you can see. None of them would believe that voice on the telephone. Where's Kitty, indeed! What a joke!

"Are you all right?" she whispered.

"Of course, Mummy. You only just left me."

"I know. But somebody said — never mind, darling. I forgot to tell you I'm going up to London. But I'll be back in time to fetch you this afternoon." Ella turned to the teacher, smiling as steadily as possible. "I'm so sorry to interrupt your class like this. There was something I had forgotten to tell Kitty."

"That's all right, Mrs. Simpson. Back to your seats, children. Not so much noise."

She wished there were not so much noise ringing in her head as she walked out of the school, across the playground, out of the gates to the parked car and the busy road — and the eyes watching her, because somewhere the man in the dark glasses would be observing the effects of his macabre joke.

The telephone *had* rung, she told herself. Mrs. Ingram could vouch for that. But she had thought it a wrong number, so there was no corroborative proof about the voice and the question.

I'll ring Doctor Greave and make an appointment when I get home, Ella decided. I really do need a tonic, if nothing else.

Partridge had arrived and was standing on the back doorstep talking to Mrs. Ingram. Ella caught Mrs. Ingram's words as she went in. "She's backwards and forwards like a yo-yo. Mr. Simpson's that worried about her. He had a word with me on the telephone yesterday. Told me to keep an eye on her. Take picking all them flowers, for instance."

"That's right, Mrs. Ingram. You could have knocked me down when I saw my garden stripped."

"Good morning, Partridge," Ella said firmly, coming into the kitchen.

The two heads separated guiltily. Partridge mumbled, "Morning, Mrs. Simpson. Nice day."

Mrs. Ingram darted to the stove.

"The coffee's still hot, Mrs. Simpson. Will you have a cup? You look fair done in. Don't she, Mr. Partridge?"

Ella sat down at the kitchen table before Mrs. Ingram should notice that her legs were bowing beneath her, like pieces of string.

"Thank you, Mrs. Ingram. I'd like some coffee. The heat's getting me down a bit. I wonder how much longer it will go on."

"Until weekend," Partridge said. He was economical with words. "Better get the hose out. Them sweet peas...."

He trundled off, and Mrs. Ingram began fussing over Ella like a skinny mother cat with a recalcitrant kitten.

"Now you drink that down, Mrs. Simpson, and then I'd say you ought to have a good lie-down. I'll answer the telephone if it rings."

"No, I'll do that."

Mrs. Ingram gave her a sideways suspicious glance. "I thought it seemed to upset you."

Ella put two liberal teaspoons of sugar in her coffee. She didn't take sugar usually, but she thought it would give her energy. She was extraordinarily tired after that scare and that crazy rush to Kitty's school. The strange thing was that she didn't want to hurry to the telephone and report it to Max. Even if he believed her, which he probably wouldn't, his concern would be useless, and too late.

"Mrs. Ingram, what did my husband say to you about me?"

Mrs. Ingram clattered the breakfast dishes defensively.

"You can't blame him, dear, he's worried about you. Says you've been doing funny things. I've noticed that, I must say."

Vague anger stirred in Ella, and died. She was too tired.

"Whatever I do has a good reason." (Those trips to the old house to indulge in her fantasy?) "Well, a reason that makes sense to me. But I do intend to see the doctor."

"You do that, dear." Mrs. Ingram was growing altogether too motherly. "That's what Mr. Simpson was going on about. You make an appointment as soon as you've drunk your coffee."

Ella nodded meekly. "All right." She really did intend to do that, but the telephone, with its uncanny private life, got in first. It rang just as she was about to dial

Doctor Greave's number.

Not allowing herself a moment for apprehension, she snatched up the receiver.

"Is that Mrs. Simpson?"

The serious courteous voice was not that of her persecutor. Relief was intoxicating.

"Yes, this is Mrs. Simpson speaking."

"I'm afraid I have bad news for you, Mrs. Simpson. Could you come to St. Anthony's Hospital in Chelsea? Your husband has had a car accident."

"Oh, God!"

"You'll come at once?" The telephone clicked.

No one, the small functioning part of Ella's mind thought irrelevantly, could accuse her of talking for an unnecessarily long time on the telephone. Her callers, with their shattering news, always rang off abruptly, leaving her standing on the edge of a precipice.

"What is it now?" came Mrs. Ingram's voice, inquisitive but plainly long-suffering.

Ella could scarcely get the words out.

"Max! In a car crash. I have to go to St. Anthony's Hospital in Chelsea."

She had grabbed her handbag and was at the door.

"I'll take the car. I'll telephone you." Halfway out she turned. "If I'm not back in time for Kitty, could you stay and get her? Or ask Mr. Bramwell?"

Mrs. Ingram hadn't had time to say a single word. She just stood in the doorway, her mouth open, her hands held up in a flapping movement, as Ella backed the car out, dangerously fast, and was off.

Half an hour's reckless drive — no watching for green Minis this time — the car parked on a yellow line, and then a breathless rush into the casualty department of the hospital. Was that where one made inquiries? She didn't know.

The girl at the desk, white-uniformed and apparently competent, said she had no record of a Mr. Simpson.

"Has he just been brought in?"

"Yes. I was telephoned. I'm his wife. They told me to come at once. He's been in a car crash."

"Oh. There was someone brought in from a car crash a little while ago. Wait a minute. Go and sit down."

Ella did so, perching on the edge of a chair, noticing vaguely that she was surrounded by other anxious people, and various minor casualties, a small boy with a tear-streaked face and a clumsily bandaged hand, a girl hobbling on a grossly swollen ankle, someone being pushed in a wheelchair. There was a murmur of low conversation. Behind a closed door a baby was crying with a high terrified sound. A stretcher was wheeled past, on it a supine body with a yellow old man's face. Two very young nurses giggled over something and hurried off.

Another stretcher, accompanied by a nurse and a hospital orderly, came by, paused. The figure on it was heavily bandaged about the head. One could see only a tuft of dark springing hair, the tip of a bluish cyanosed nose.

Max!

Ella was hanging over the unconscious form exclaiming, "My husband! Is he badly hurt? Is he dying?"

The nurse looked surprised. So did the orderly.

"You'd better go around to reception,

madam. This patient hasn't been identified."

"But they said — they rang me — my husband, Max Simpson, had been brought in."

"Then this can't be him because he's unidentified. See?"

But Ella was unconvinced. Her gaze lingered fearfully on the still figure. Max's handsome face ruined, his sharp intelligent eyes hidden by all those bandages not watching her anymore. . . .

"Is he — dead?"

The nurse looked outraged. How could this silly woman be so stupid as to think they would be wasting time on a corpse? The damaged face so carefully bandaged, the red blanket neatly tucked in at the sides, the hands, unmarked, lying on top of it. Square pale hands with a slight dark furring of hair on their backs.

Not Max's hands! Definitely not Max's hands, which were long, bony and hairless.

The stretcher moved on. The orderly looked back and winked at Ella. And then she knew that the whole thing was another nightmare, quite unreal, another ghastly hoax perpetrated by her unknown tormentor.

Nevertheless, she found her way to the main reception desk where, on making her inquiry, she was received with mild surprise.

"But, Mrs. Simpson, it wouldn't be the hospital who informed you of an accident, it would be the police. They always send someone around to break the news. So your husband couldn't be here, could he?"

Kind eyes looked at her, assessing her distress.

"Can't you ring your husband's office and find out? There's a telephone over there."

Fabritex's number. She could remember it, by some miracle. Her brain still had a minimum of functioning power. Max's secretary, Penny, bright, pleasant, impersonal.

"Bad luck, Mrs. Simpson. You've just missed him."

"How long since he went out?"

"Oh, not five minutes ago."

It was, Ella calculated laboriously, almost an hour since that horrible call had been made. And all the time Max had been sitting in his office, dictating to Penny, chatting, having his morning coffee.

"He'll be back early this afternoon, Mrs. Simpson. Shall I ask him to ring you?"

"No, thank you," Ella said.

She didn't want Max to ring her, she realized. She simply didn't know how to talk to him about this.

"All right, Mrs. Simpson?" asked the nice girl at the reception desk.

"Yes, thank you. It's been a mistake."

"Well, isn't that lucky!"

Lucky? Yes, she supposed it was.

But unlucky for that poor unidentified patient disguised with bandages. Unlucky for his wife who would have to hang over him trying to recognize him, trying to decide if she still loved him. . . .

Ella didn't remember anything of the drive home. She found herself sitting behind the wheel of the Rover outside her house without any knowledge of how she had got there.

Someone was opening the door and helping her out. A man's square pale hand with a dark sprinkling of hairs on its back.

She cried out, seeing the bandaged figure again, the unfamiliar undamaged hands lying on the red blanket.

"Hold up, Mrs. Simpson, darling. Let's get you inside."

Dear Mr. Brontë, always there in time of trouble. She gave a feeble laugh.

"Have you and Mrs. Ingram been getting together?" And then she subsided into his arms, as if they were a downy feather bed, full of comforting darkness.

By the time Doctor Greave arrived she had quite recovered. The taste of brandy lingered in her mouth, and her tiredness was more acute, so that she felt she never wanted to leave the couch or the darkened room again, but she was perfectly compos mentis.

Wasn't she?

"There was a mistake," she repeated patiently. "It must have been another Mr. Simpson in an accident. It wasn't Max. But I got a terrible shock. There was this bandaged figure and I thought it was Max until I saw his hands."

And I felt no grief. Shock but no grief. . . .

Doctor Greave unwound the constricting bandage from her upper arm. "Blood pressure a bit low," he said. "You're suffering from shock. You'll need to rest."

"Nobody believes what I tell them!" Ella exclaimed.

"No? Have you been feeling tired lately, Mrs. Simpson? Had difficulty in concentrating?"

"Only this week. I've found the heat a bit much."

"I think we all have. We're not used to it, are we? But I think you could do with a checkup. Come and see me next week."

"Has my husband been talking to you?" Ella asked suspiciously.

"No, but it would be fair enough if he had. I think you're having a little very natural depression after miscarrying. Get your woman to make you a cup of tea, and then take this" — he placed a small red pill on the table beside her — "and sleep for the rest of the day. Then you'll be in a better state to welcome your husband home. Eh, my dear?"

Doctor Greave was kindly, but quite imperceptive. He was splendid for women having successful full-time pregnancies, but for her, bewildered and battered and lost, he was no use at all.

How could she just take a little red pill and sleep when there was Kitty to protect from some unknown menace, when at any moment the telephone might ring with a new ingenious form of torture, when she must be wide awake when Max came home in order to relate calmly and intelligently what had happened?

Including the revealing moment when she had known that she was not grief-stricken? That would depend on how Max behaved to her, whether she would want to be vindictive. *What has happened to you, Ella, who once never knew what vindictiveness was?*

"You must take this pill, Ella."

Was that Booth here still, interfering in his perfectly well-meaning way?

"I can't. I have to stay awake to fetch Kitty."

"I'll fetch Kitty."

"You! But — "

"She knows me. She won't object."

"No, but — "

"Stop saying 'but' and swallow this."

"Tell her for once she'll have to do without bringing Sam home. He's too energetic."

"Right. Sam can go and break his heart. Take the pill, Ella, darling."

Ella, darling. . . . Why did that sound so much more intimate than the casual joking Mrs. Simpson, darling? Although actually she liked both forms of endearment. It was nice for a half-crazy woman to still get endearments. Booth had perception. Much more than Doctor Greave. Much more than Max. She didn't know him well, but that was a thing she recognized at once. Even if Booth had to tell her that she was a little out of her mind he would do it with the greatest tact.

Chapter 12

When Ella opened her eyes Kitty was sitting on the floor in the corner of the room playing with her dolls which were propped up in various places. They were a crippled derelict lot even without the bandages that now decorated their heads and limbs. But Kitty, crooning over them lovingly, was almost capable of conjuring real smiles from their wooden and plastic faces.

"You have to take your medicine and rest," Ella heard her busy voice. "And you mustn't cry or you'll wake my mother. She's very tired. That's why your father wasn't allowed to come today. But he'll come tomorrow and take us for a walk."

Ella found that after all she was able to smile again. If she just watched Kitty with her falling curtain of blond hair, surrounded by the strange little family, her heart became full of calm and love.

But someone else was in the room. A figure stood over her.

"Would you like some tea? Or a cold drink? I don't recommend alcohol on top of a sedative."

"Booth! You're still here. Do you have to be my nurse now? How awful for you."

"It has its advantages. For instance I've just been made first grandfather to an assorted collection of children. How many, Kitty?"

Kitty looked anxious.

"Is eleven too many?"

"A very satisfying number, I'd say."

"Booth, you are kind," Ella said. She clung to her drowsiness which made things vague and endurable. "Why is Kitty playing hospitals?"

"A sudden epidemic, I believe. But with modern drugs all will be well."

Kitty smiled radiantly at Booth. He went on, "Not that fresh air isn't a great healer. What about a short airing for the family, Kitty?"

Kitty considered, then agreed, and began

arranging the dolls in the pram with due care given to bandaged limbs. Ella's drowsiness became less muffling.

"Don't let her go far. Kitty, stay right on the patio."

"Oh, Mummy, you're fussing again. Sam said you were fussing when you came to school this morning."

"Did you go to school?" Booth asked with interest. "I didn't know."

"Yes, I did. I had to. Run along, Kitty."

After an interminable arranging and rearranging of her pram load Kitty trundled off, and Ella reluctantly brought herself back to the painful present.

"Has the telephone rung this afternoon?"

"No."

"Are you sure?"

"Perfectly. Unless both Mrs. Ingram and I have become suddenly deaf."

Ella sighed. "Thank God for that."

"Then go on. Tell me why you went to Kitty's school."

It seemed an immeasurable time since the morning, although the memory of her panic was all too vivid.

"I had this telephone call saying,

'Where's Kitty?' Nothing else. Just 'Where's Kitty?' So what could I do but rush off to school to see if she was all right? She was perfectly all right, of course, and everyone stared at me. The teacher couldn't think why I was in such a state. But lately Max has been dinning into me never to be late for Kitty. I think he'd got an idea that she might be kidnapped, though goodness knows why, since we aren't rich people. Or picked up by a man and raped, perhaps. He's terribly nervous about her."

"Hasn't he always been?"

"No, he's never fussed like this. It's as if Mrs. Gibson's kidnapping has put ideas in his head. Or else he's had some sort of scare he doesn't want to tell me about. He doesn't think I'm up to much at present." Her voice ended wearily.

"And after you found Kitty well at school. What happened then?"

"I'd scarcely got in when the telephone rang again and it was this call from the hospital about Max. I completely panicked then, and got in the car and flew. But it was nothing but a stupid hoax. You know, I've been thinking it's very strange that this man only rings when I'm here to answer. Mrs. Ingram says the telephone never rings when she's here alone. It's as if I'm being watched and he knows exactly when to catch me. So no one else has heard his voice, and no one really believes me."

"I believe you, Ella."

Gratitude rushed through her.

"I *couldn't* make up a horrible hoax like that about Max having an accident, could I? My subconscious couldn't want my husband badly hurt. Or dead." Her eyes were full of remembered shock and guilt.

"One's subconscious is weird and wonderful, but not quite that weird and wonderful. Ella, now don't you think you ought to call in the police?"

"Max says they'd laugh at me."

They would say, "Hey, there's that goofy Mrs. Simpson hearing her voices again. Who does she think we are, headshrinkers?"

"I don't think they'd laugh at you. At least, they could put a tap on the line. This looks like a deliberate campaign."

"I know," she agreed reluctantly. "Max has someone getting at him in the evenings, too, but that's business. It's tied up with who gets this new job, and it will stop when the announcement is made."

"That's what he tells you."

"It's true enough. I know Max."

"Do you think your calls might be part of the same thing?"

"I suppose they could be. But they're so kinky. I keep thinking they're to do with something much more serious than Max's job. As if someone is trying to destroy me," she confessed with a feeling of shame. "That's a classic case of persecution complex, Max says."

"Ella, don't you realize that the very fact you're able to discuss this proves you're absolutely sane?"

"It doesn't prove anything. How do I know I'm not imagining what's said on the telephone? Why do I keep thinking I'm being followed and watched?"

"Perhaps you actually are being followed and watched."

"You didn't believe that yesterday when we had lunch and the man in the dark glasses was there. "

"Perhaps my skepticism is wearing down.

Would you like me to have a talk with the police?"

"Oh, no!" Her reaction was full of the familiar panic. "Don't do that. Max would be furious."

"Why?" Booth asked uncompromisingly.

"He just would be. I told you. He's so afraid they'll think me just another nut case. And how's that going to look for the new export manager of a firm as important as Fabritex? Pretty shaming."

"Ella, what sort of a husband have you got? What sort of a marriage?"

She evaded his serious regard. "Don't let's start discussing my marriage at this stage. And who are you to talk, anyway?"

"I'm not setting myself up as a perfect husband. I don't suppose I'd recognize a good marriage if I saw one." Ella squirmed uncomfortably beneath his probing eyes. He was beginning to dissect her like one of his plays.

"Did you ask Max about the mink coat?"

"Jacket. Yes. He said he knew nothing about it. It was a wicked trumped-up story."

"Told by whom?"

"He said he didn't know, but I think he does know. It's a business rival."

"The one who's getting at him on the telephone?"

"I expect so. Really, big business — sometimes you'd be just as honest being a burglar."

"So you got nowhere about the mink jacket, and now you have another problem for him tonight. Because if you're not going to tell the police you've got to tell your husband and let him do something about it. Repeat to him word for word what those telephone conversations were, especially the one about the accident and the hospital."

"Word for word — I don't think I can remember — " She frowned. She simply had no stamina nowadays. Already her mind was blurring again. "I was so shocked I didn't take it in properly. I heard the name of the hospital and that was about all. But I do know it wasn't the same voice speaking."

"Not the one that said, 'Where's Kitty?' "

"No."

"He could have been disguising it, of course."

"Yes. Perhaps. I didn't think of that. And

257

now you see, because you're here, the telephone never rings. As if he knows."

"Pity. I'd like to talk to him."

"It wouldn't be any use. He'd just hang up. By the way, isn't it getting late? Don't you have to go to London?"

"When Lorna gets home. She'll stay with you then."

Ella's tired body was still capable of feeling tingles of alarm.

"Then you truly are alarmed about what's going on?"

"Curious."

"You think I shouldn't be alone?"

"Neither you nor Kitty. Babes in the wood."

That description suddenly made her remember something else, the Sleeping Beauty garden this morning, and the surprising plume of smoke from the chimney.

"Booth, I forgot to tell you. Someone lit a fire in Edith's house early this morning. I saw the smoke."

"Could you be sure, from such a distance?"

"Oh, yes. It was a beautiful clear dawn.

Anyway, I drove over to see, after I'd taken Kitty to school. Someone had been there, and lit a fire in the ballroom. But whoever he was, he'd swept up the ashes and left it quite tidy. Don't you think that was funny?"

He hadn't seemed to be listening, his expression was so far away.

"Very," he said at last. "Very funny."

Then the doorbell rang and Ella heard Lorna Bramwell's voice. She had got the note Booth had left for her, and wanted to know what was going on.

"Get her husband home, why don't you?" Ella heard her say.

Ella jumped up and made her string legs carry her to the door.

"No, you mustn't do that. Max would be rather angry."

He already thinks his wife is being a bind, a pain in the neck, and a distinct hindrance to his future. . . .

"I mean, I'm perfectly all right. After all, I'm all in one piece. I'm not like that poor man on the stretcher."

"Ella has been the victim of a particularly nasty hoax," Booth explained. "She's a bit nervous, understandably. Make her some tea, Lorna, and answer the telephone if it rings. Keep an eye on Kitty, too."

"Sure," said Lorna, good-naturedly. "Like to tell me more about these suburban excitements?"

"When I get home. Don't bother Ella about it. She's supposed to be resting."

"I offered to baby-sit, not to hold Mamma's hand." Lorna's smile was jollier, less inhibited, than Booth's. "But I don't mind doing that. I thought Collingham was going to be an excruciatingly dull place, but already we have stolen cars, kidnappings, hoaxes or practical jokes or whatever. It's certainly more interesting than grubbing among dusty books all day. How do you like your tea, Ella? And do you really want me to answer the telephone if it rings?"

"No," said Ella tensely.

"Yes," said Booth, departing. "Stand no nonsense, Lorna."

"Goodness, he's getting bossy," said Lorna. "What have you done to him? He's the mildest creature, usually. That's why that bitch Rosalie hurt him so much."

"Did she?"

"You can be sure she did. I don't know

why he fell for her in the first place, but he did. I suppose your problem is men, too?"

"Well, yes. At least these people getting at me are men. Yesterday and the day before I just imagined I was being watched. Today it was real."

Lorna looked at her keenly, but asked no questions.

"Lots of odd types about nowadays. I blame all this drugging."

"Someone's trying to drive me mad," Ella said flatly.

"Goodness! Well, now." Lorna was like an old-fashioned nanny, unaffected by melodrama. "Don't let him succeed, eh? Shall I call Kitty in, or shall we have our tea outdoors? Let's go outdoors. It's so hot, no wonder it's difficult to think straight."

"But I am thinking straight," Ella said later, when the tea had been drunk and Kitty had returned to her dolls, and the sun was a great red peony away in the distance, hanging over the dark trees and the old house.

Because the suspicion had drifted into her mind that Max might just possibly be joining in with her unknown persecutor in this amusing game of making poor Ella mad. Well, not violently mad, but just vaguely loony. Booth had once asked her tentatively if she thought her husband might be making these calls, but she had rejected the idea in astonishment. Now she knew she was not entirely sure.

If Max wasn't joining, she fancied he wasn't objecting to the game.

Or was this sudden suspicion another symptom of mental instability? She had been vague enough lately to drive Max up the wall.

"Lorna, I've forgotten to do the shopping again!" she cried, pressing her hands together, perspiration breaking out all over her. "Oh, heavens, what will Max say? And what am I to give him to eat?"

"Make him take you out to dinner. Good excuse. I'll give Kitty some supper."

Ella shook her head.

"I don't think either of us is in the mood. Max will be tired. He's been on tenterhooks all this week about a new job. I think there's been a bit of a palace revolution going on in the firm that he won't tell me about.

Psychiatrists talk about the stress of modern life. I don't know."

"Well, a couple of centuries ago it would have been into the Tower and off with his head. Some stress then, too, I imagine. We're not much better than animals, the way we prey on each other. Take that kidnapping, for instance, that wretched woman who was unlucky enough to have a husband with more or less unlimited wealth."

"Was? You think she's dead?"

"Sure of it. Those chaps can be as clever as monkeys, but they panic fast. They don't want an articulate witness. Oh, sorry, Ella. I didn't mean to talk about gloomy things. Well, what's for supper, if you won't persuade your husband to take you out? Shall I concoct something? I'm crazy about cooking but I don't get much opportunity with Booth out most evenings."

Ella came to the door.

"Would you really like to? Can I come in the kitchen and watch?"

"It's hot out here."

"It's comfortable. Nice smells, nice ordinary things. We had a big kitchen in our house and I used to watch Cook."

"Have you always been homesick?" Lorna asked, offhandedly, her head in Ella's store cupboard.

"I suppose I have a bit, although I didn't really realize it until Kitty and I found that old house."

"You're not exactly a suburbanite, are you?"

"No. I'm not one at all. I should have done more with this house. But we won't be here much longer. Max says we'll have to live in the stockbroker belt if he gets this job."

"Will you like that any better?"

Ella looked out of the window at the neatly shaved lawn, the geometric flower beds.

"I always wanted a wild garden. If I could have that — but Max likes order. He has a passion for it. That's one reason he didn't mind about my losing my baby. Babies are chronically untidy little pests."

"Myself, I prefer books," Lorna said, and Ella knew she was referring to marriage, not babies. "Oh, with some involvement now and then, of course. I must say your Kitty makes one think of what one has missed."

"It's nice to have you here," Ella said impulsively. "You and Booth."

"Except if you move into deepest Surrey. Well, now, I've decided on a cheese soufflé, salad and fruit. I'll make myself scarce when your husband gets home, so you'll have to time the soufflé and take it out of the oven. Okay?"

"Thank you, Lorna. Even my poor brain can remember that much."

Lorna gave her a sharp look.

"There's nothing wrong with your brain, if I may say so. Brainwashing, maybe, not brain damage."

"You — think so?"

"That's what I said. That's what my brother said, too."

So that was what Booth was thinking. Poor brainwashed Mrs. Simpson who must be rather charming in her right mind.

"But *why?*" Ella asked desperately.

"You'll have to find out, won't you?" Lorna said levelly. "And the sooner the better."

"Am I being brainwashed?" Ella demanded of Max, for he had hardly been home five minutes and listened to her story which now sounded completely fantastic before he began giving her his sideways suspicious glance. The all-too-familiar woolliness came over her.

He was horrified by what she had told him. Not because she had been the victim of a hoax, but because of her own behavior. How could she be so gullible, so naive, running about like a mad thing? Anyone with normal common sense would have made a few judicious telephone calls and established the hoax.

"How could I have been in an accident when I didn't have the car?" he demanded. "Didn't you even think of that?"

She felt bruised by his insensitivity.

"I thought someone else must have been driving you."

"But I'd have been in the office at that time. You'd have realized that if you had stopped to think."

"I didn't stop to think!" Ella cried. "Would you have stopped to think if you had been told that I was in an accident?"

Max had the grace to look ashamed. He also looked overwhelmingly tired, the lines grooved deep in a now-permanently harassed face. What was happening to him, to them both?

"Maybe not. But it's all right now. You've got over it, haven't you? You didn't need to get that pally with the next-door neighbors. Told them everything, I expect?"

"Why not? I collapsed. Don't you care about that?"

"Of course I care, Ella, but they don't know your state of mind like I do."

"No," said Ella coldly. "Booth was more concerned in getting the police than in my state of mind."

He was unable to repress a flash of alarm. "You didn't let him!"

"Would it worry you so much if I had?"

"Ella, don't be so daft. Police at this stage in my life — that's sure to be misconstrued. No one will believe it's because my wife has been dumb enough to be taken in by a practical joke. I admit it was nasty — "

"Nastier than you think!" Ella retorted, provoked to sudden hot anger. "Because I found I didn't care if you had been in an accident." Her voice was rising. "I didn't care if that bandaged man was you. I simply didn't care!"

"Ella!"

"That's what this brainwashing is doing to me. Because I may be in a peculiar mental state, but it's a deliberately induced one. At least" — again the awful uncertainty came over her — "I think so."

"Is that what this interfering egghead next door has been saying to you? He's a critic, isn't he? All critics are destructive."

"That isn't fair! You don't even know him."

"Nor do I want to. I just don't want him interfering in our lives."

"Then you mustn't leave me alone all day with that damned telephone ringing."

Max decided on a change of mood. His face became concerned and tender. She was almost taken in. She almost relaxed in his arms when he put them around her. But in the last few days he had given her too many lessons in suspicion. Now she couldn't trust his motives. His change of expression was too calculated.

"Ella, love! Try just another day. For my sake. I've told you I'm sure it's only someone getting at me through you. That's if you're absolutely certain you heard all that nonsense accurately."

She drew away sharply. He had ruined her belief in his concern for her by that last sentence. It seemed he would rather discredit her sanity than that of her persecutors.

If there were persecutors. . . .

"It's no use, Max," she said wearily. "I don't know what's happening to us, and I can't trust you to tell me, because you don't tell the truth. Perhaps you're going to explain someday. I don't know. I'm not sure I care very much."

He turned away for a moment, surprised and alarmed; she thought that he was going to burst into tears. But eventually he composed his face, and said, almost as wearily as she had spoken, "Just one more day. Then we'll have a happy weekend, whether I get that damn job or not. By the way, did you buy your dress? No, I suppose you didn't," he finished, lamely.

What did he think her powers of

recuperation were? How much did he know her, after six years of intimacy? How much had he ever tried to know her?

"I'll get the supper," she said. "Lorna's left a soufflé cooking. It will be ready in about six minutes. I'll just call Kitty in."

"I want to watch the news."

"Then you'll have to watch it while you eat, or the soufflé will be ruined."

"Okay. Let's do that."

He watched attentively but was obviously disappointed. Something he had wanted to hear wasn't mentioned. Mrs. Gibson's kidnapping? He got up and turned off the television, and finished his food silently. When Kitty spoke to him, he didn't hear, and she complained, "Daddy, you're awfully deaf."

"Daddy's worried, darling," Ella said, then wished she hadn't because Kitty let the curtain of blond hair fall over her face in her typical gesture of withdrawal. Poor vulnerable Kitty with both parents behaving so strangely. No wonder she turned to her uninhibited friend Sam.

Half an hour later, just after Kitty had gone upstairs to bed, the telephone rang.

The way Max leaped to answer it suggested that he had been expecting the call, and was eager to get it.

He was in such a hurry that this time he forgot to pull the door shut after him, and Ella could hear distinctly when his voice dropped with disappointment.

"Yes, fine, fine. We're all well. . . . Ella's feeling the heat a bit. . . . Yes, much too hot. It almost gives you hallucinations — no, I didn't mean anything by that. . . . Wait a minute, I'll get Ella." He laid down the receiver. "Ella, your mother."

"Oh!" Her voice fell, too. Usually she enjoyed a long gossip with her mother, but just now it was going to be difficult to keep up a facade of untroubled normality. She would have to blame the heat, as Max had already done for her.

Her mother, it seemed, thought that they should get out of town for the weekend. "Nasty polluted air," she said. She was waging a campaign against pollution. "It's terribly bad for Kitty. Must be twice as bad in this heat wave. Bring her down, and let her breathe our clean air."

Ella saw Max shaking his head at her,

and made feeble excuses. Personally, she longed to get into the car with Kitty, and drive fast into the clean country air her mother talked about. The vision in her mind was gone as quickly as it had come. But it hadn't included Max. Just her and Kitty. . . .

"Is she on about the air again?" Max grumbled.

Ella nodded. "It's true, I suppose."

"Well, we'll be moving out of polluted areas soon, too. Didn't you tell her that? Haven't you got faith in me?"

He looked so indignant that Ella had to say loyally, "Of course I have." As far as acquiring a new job and a new status were concerned, she did have faith in him. He was more than capable of doing that. At any cost.

From then on the evening dragged. Max was unable to settle to the newspaper, the television, or even the usually absorbing business reports which he carried home in his briefcase. He seemed to be waiting for the telephone to ring again. He kept lifting his head and listening. He had caught her nerves about it.

Ella, sitting in the open doorway, tried to lose herself in the peace of the evening. It was still faintly daylight. The air was warm and utterly still and smelled of flowers from the garden, with an undercurrent of gasoline fumes. The pollution about which her mother had a fixation.

The garden at the old house, she thought, would smell only of night-scented stock, tobacco plant, evening primroses. Old-fashioned ragged flowers that didn't appeal to Max's passion for tidiness.

Hollyhocks, red-hot poker, antirrhinums. . . . She looked around and saw that Max had turned on the television again, and was sitting with his hands locked together, obviously not watching what was on the screen.

"Why don't you go to bed?" Ella asked. "You look as if you've had it today. Even more than I have."

"In a minute. I want to see the news."

"You watched it earlier."

"What if I did? Things go on happening."

"What are you expecting to hear, Max? News of Mrs. Gibson?"

Now what had made her say that? For

even while Max was saying vehemently, "Good God, no! Why should I be worrying about her?" she had seen the revealing look on his face, the shock and the flicker of fear.

"Not that one isn't interested in her being found," he added carefully. "And alive and well."

"But without any clothes." Again the words came unexpectedly from her lips, and were as startling to her as to Max.

"Now what on earth makes you say that, Ella?"

"I don't know. I just had a sudden picture — you know my funny mind — " She shook her head bemusedly. She didn't care herself for these random thoughts that flew into her head. "Because they couldn't let her be identified by her clothes, could they?"

"She won't need to be identified," Max said harshly. "She'll arrive back home or walk into a police station. I wish you'd stop harping on Mrs. Gibson. Where do you get these crazy ideas, anyway?"

"I hope they are crazy. I certainly hope they are."

The news lacked any sensational item, fortunately, but Max seemed disappointed, as if he had wanted to go to bed with echoes of some disaster ringing in his head.

He hesitated by the telephone before going upstairs, as if he were willing it to ring. But it didn't, and his shoulders slumped as he climbed the stairs.

He seemed very tired. He was miles away from her. Unreachable. And she was no longer so much frightened as puzzled and sad.

Why didn't he confide in her, tell her what was worrying him, make love to her? Because he thought her mind incapable of intelligent understanding, and her body of response?

Oh, to hell with it. . . .

It was Max who had the nightmare that night. He began thrashing about and muttering something unintelligible. He seemed as if he were struggling physically with his own private tormentor, for he grunted and finally gave a muffled cry.

Ella shook him awake.

"What are you doing?" he mumbled.

"You were having a nightmare. You were fighting somebody, I think."

"Oh? It's gone now." He sat up, rubbing his head, then held it in his hands as if he were reliving the nightmare he said he couldn't remember.

Ella pleaded, "You know you're worried about something. Why don't you tell me what's going on? If someone's blackmailing you why don't you go to the police?"

"And destroy us?"

Us, he said. Not just himself, and his position with the firm.

The dampness of perspiration on Ella's face and shoulders turned cold. "But what can you be blackmailed about? That mink jacket?"

He sprang abruptly out of bed.

"I didn't say I was being blackmailed, and I told you there was no mink jacket. I'm going down for a drink. Want one?"

Ella curled up on her pillow. "No, thank you."

When he came back, a long time later, she had been half dozing. She felt him get in beside her, and when he put his arms around her smelled the whiskey on his breath.

He had drowned his sorrows, for now his embrace was tight and loving. "Sorry, Ella.

Sorry, love," he kept mumbling into her hair.

Poor Max, for some reason which it seemed he was never going to tell her, had been going through hell, too.

But feeling the weight of his head on her breast, and seeing the dark outline of it, Ella remembered the bandaged figure in the hospital, and the small cold griefless core of her heart.

She felt a little compassion now, because she was a naturally compassionate person. But that was all she did feel.

Chapter 13

In the morning Ella slept heavily, and woke to find Max fully dressed, standing over her.

"I've given Kitty her breakfast, but you'd better hurry if you're going to get her to school on time."

Ella struggled up, her tired limbs almost refusing to move.

"Why didn't you wake me sooner?"

"You were tired. You needed the rest."

Not that old litany again. Had he forgotten his own vulnerability in the night? Would he say she had dreamed it?

Had she dreamed it?

"Is it just as hot?" she asked, reaching for her robe.

"More so. The kitchen thermometer says eighty degrees already. So don't rush about. Why don't you go back to bed when you come back from taking Kitty?"

"I'm not ill," Ella said irritably, then abandoned that useless argument. "I'm sorry, did you get your own breakfast?"

"Not to worry. I didn't want much. I'm off now." He had the morning paper tucked under his arm. He didn't usually take the paper to work.

Poor darling, he couldn't have had time to read it, what with getting Kitty's breakfast and all.

"Oh, and another thing, if the telephone rings, let Mrs. Ingram answer it."

"But he won't talk to her."

"He?"

"You know who I mean. This man with the evil voice."

"Who I'm sure only talks inside your head, love. Really." Max was using his gentle humorous persuasive voice, his soft-sell voice, that was so eminently successful in business. And also in his private life, until this perplexing week.

Now she wasn't sure she was ever going to trust it again.

"All right," she said wearily. "I'll let Mrs. Ingram answer the telephone."

"Good girl. Then I'm off. Wish me luck."

Of course, today was the day the announcement would be made about the new job.

"Fabritex, the multimillion textile firm, announces the appointment of Mr. Max Simpson to the position of export manager for Europe. . . ."

Poor Max, she was showing less than a wifely interest. It just couldn't be helped.

While she was brushing Kitty's hair she had another of her uncomfortable random thoughts. Was there something in the morning paper that Max hadn't wanted her to see? Well, she could soon find that out. She could buy another paper.

"Mummy, are you sick today?"

Kitty's concerned and tender eyes seemed to expect anything. Ella hugged her, and laughed. She had always laughed a lot with Kitty, knowing children loved gaiety.

"No, I'm quite better."

"So's my family," Kitty said at once, in relief. "Can Sam come this afternoon?"

While answering yes, Ella was deciding that she wouldn't buy a paper after all. Whatever was in it, she was almost certain she would be happier not knowing.

This was an opinion, however, to which Mrs. Ingram didn't subscribe.

Discarding her shiny mackintosh and revealing her meager figure in a red dress with black spots (like a neat little ladybird), Mrs. Ingram said with a certain amount of macabre enjoyment, "Fancy that naked body in the river!"

Ella's heart jolted.

"What naked body? A man's?"

"No, a woman's. Age between twenty-five and thirty-five, white, no identifying marks." Mrs. Ingram was quoting with relish.

"A prostitute," Ella murmured.

"Mrs. Daphne Gibson," said Mrs. Ingram. "That's what they think."

No clothes! No clothes! No clothes!

"That poor husband has to go and identify the body. But mark my words — they wretches — "

"Where?" Ella got out.

"Miles from here, dear. Don't look so upset. Down near the docks. Reckon they hoped she'd be taken out to sea on the tide."

"How — how clumsy!"

"Amatoors!" Mrs. Ingram said scathingly.

"So she must have been dead practically all the time," Ella said in horror.

"Didn't I always say so?"

And that was what Max had read in the paper this morning, and had concealed from her. Indeed, that was what he must have been waiting to hear on the news last night.

Had he privately known about it already? Was that why he had hated her having that intuition that Mrs. Gibson had no clothes?

"Mrs. Simpson, I declare, you don't look so good still. You shouldn't take these things to heart. They ain't nothing to do with you."

"No, of course not," Ella said as firmly as possible. She had to believe that, hadn't she, if she were to remain sane?

The sanity of the witness, Mrs. Ella Simpson, has been called in doubt by her husband, and by her doctor who had urged her to come for a checkup....

"I think we both need a good cup of coffee," said Mrs. Ingram cheerfully. "You goin' shopping today, Mrs. Simpson? I declare, I don't know what you're feeding your poor husband on these days, your store cupboard's mighty low."

"It might not *be* Mrs. Gibson," she said.

"I'll take a bet, if you like. Mr. Partridge now, he'll have a bet with me. He likes betting on unusual subjects."

"You're a pair of ghouls," Ella cried, and heard Mrs. Ingram's good-natured laughter as she hurried inevitably into the garden to look up for Booth's dark head at the window next door.

It wasn't at the window, but it must have been somewhere else watching, for almost at once Booth emerged from the back door and came to the dividing fence.

"Morning, Ella. How are you?"

"What do you think of the news?"

"About Mrs. Gibson? Expected."

"You think it's really her?"

"Afraid so."

"Mrs. Ingram thinks so, too. Not Max, though. He always said Mrs. Gibson would arrive home alive and well. But he did take the paper to work so I wouldn't read it. That was a bit silly, because I'd have known sooner or later.

"He probably didn't want me to be alone

all day thinking about it," she added defensively. "He knew I'd let that kidnapping get on my mind. I mean, what with those telephone calls and the men I thought were watching me. Bad things seem to get mixed up together in one's mind. Like a sort of horrid sludge."

"And do you think the bad things will be over now?"

"Because they've found a body? But that couldn't be anything to do with us, could it? Not Max and me!"

Booth said nothing, and she didn't know what his expression meant.

"If they've found a body they'll have to find a murderer, of course." She was talking too much and too nervously. But who said her mind wasn't working? She was entirely logical. "Or murderers," she added.

"Now you sound like Mrs. Ingram."

"Yes, I do, don't I?" She reflected a moment and another of her zany thoughts came out. "You know, I always had this feeling that they'd find Mrs. Gibson without any clothes. Max really does think I'm mad."

"I hope you told him everything last night."

"Yes," she said guardedly.

"And so?"

"Well, as I expected he wouldn't hear of calling the police. He said wait until after today. He'll know about the job, and then there'll be no reason for our telephone friend to go on persecuting us. If he did go on that would be an entirely different matter and I suppose something would have to be done about it. Although Max has never believed me, you know. He thinks I'm a sort of Joan of Arc, only my voices don't come from angels."

Again Booth made no comment. He was very quiet and contemplative this morning. Ella thought vaguely how things over these four hot days had changed so much. At the beginning of her acquaintance with her next-door neighbor, she had spoken loyally and defensively about her husband. Now she was no longer defending him. Indeed, she preferred not to talk about him at all.

He's frightened of something, Booth. Last night he had a nightmare. But it's only some sort of horrid blackmail over the job.

285

It's nothing, nothing, to do with Mrs. Gibson. . . .

"Lorna made us a soufflé last night," she said irrelevantly. "It was delicious. Even Kitty, whose appetite has to be tempted in this heat, ate every scrap."

"You're chattering, Mrs. Simpson."

She liked his rare twinkle.

"I'm a chatterer."

"We can't gossip like charwomen over the back fence. Am I coming over to hold your hand, or do I drive myself back to the typewriter?"

"I'm perfectly all right," Ella said. "I can't go on keeping you from your work. The telephone hasn't rung once this morning." She said that cautiously, because she already knew that that inanimate instrument had ears and a life of its own. "And anyway Max said that Mrs. Ingram was to answer it if it does ring. So I'm going to be lazy out here. What can happen in one's back garden?"

"All right, I'll go back to work. Actually, I've got a lunch appointment in the city, but I'll cancel it if you'd like me to."

"Now why should you do that for me? If

286

I'm not fit to be left alone it's Max's responsibility, not yours."

"You're getting me wrong. It's only that you look as if you haven't slept and as if you expect to find a bogeyman behind every bush."

Ella shook her head, laughing a little.

"No, I don't truly. Not today. I'm calm and composed and confident. I'm not going to look out on the street for green Minis, or green dragons, or whatever they are. And I'm not going to answer the — "

The sound of the telephone ringing in the house made instant nonsense of her claim to composure.

"Mrs. Ingram will answer it," she said breathlessly.

He wouldn't speak to Mrs. Ingram. He would hang up and ring later, when he knew she was alone. . . .

Mrs. Ingram appeared at the back door.

"It's Mr. Simpson, Mrs. Simpson. He wants to speak to you."

"Oh, Max! He must have heard about the job," Ella cried, and ran indoors.

"Ella!"

No, he hadn't heard about the job, she

knew at once. His voice was too flat and quiet.

"Yes, Max?"

"I expect you've heard about Mrs. — that body being found."

"Mrs. Ingram told me it was in the paper," Ella said pointedly.

"Yes, I read about it on the train."

Lie number one. . . .

"Ella, I only wanted to say that if the police come around, don't chatter."

Her heart jolted.

"Why would they come around?"

"They might. It's a murder hunt now. If that body is Mrs. Gibson's."

He *knows* it is, Ella thought, fear tingling down her spine.

"Might want fingerprints," he was going on. "You know how they fingerprint whole villages sometimes. Don't tell them anything you haven't told them already."

"What else is there to tell them? Oh! You mean the telephone calls."

"They wouldn't believe you, you know, the dumb way you've been going on."

"But Max!" Her voice was high with tension. "Were those calls to do with — "

"Got to go now," came Max's voice briskly, and she knew someone had come into his office. "I'll ring you this afternoon. Nothing to worry about. Bye, love."

Mrs. Ingram, deliberately working in the vicinity of the hall, said sympathetically, "Bad news, dear?"

"No. My husband only thinks the police may be making inquiries in this street again. Taking fingerprints."

"That ain't nothing," Mrs. Ingram said knowledgeably. "You don't need to get upset about that, unless you're guilty." She gave her strange little hoot of laughter. "Anyways, unless they've found some fingerprints to compare, it don't get them nowhere, does it?"

"Where would they find them?"

"Plenty of places. Some article of Mrs. Gibson's, her handbag or a shoe or something. Or they might have found the gray Jag and have kept quiet about it."

"Mrs. Ingram, you've missed your vocation," Ella said shakily. "You should have been a policewoman."

She was glad that Booth had gone home.

This had been a gray little conversation that she didn't want to repeat. Least of all could she have mentioned her private fears. Putting them into words might make them real.

When Booth predictably stuck his head out of the upstairs window she called, "Everything's all right. So go and have a nice lunch."

"You sure you'll be all right?"

"Who's sure of anything? But I'm not that feeble that I can't be left alone. Let me get back a bit of self-respect."

And thank you for everything, dear Mr. Brontë. . . .

The police, contrary to Max's expectation, didn't come. The telephone didn't ring again. The morning, apart from the occasional clatter that announced Mrs. Ingram's presence, was completely peaceful.

The heat rose, the haze deepened, the flowers wilted a little, Partridge came and said there was nothing he could do, the garden was as tidy as a well-kept drawing room. Not even weeds were growing in this weather. He departed, and shortly after midday Mrs. Ingram would depart.

That would be the test, the two hours she had to spend alone before going for Kitty. Ella was regretting that she hadn't given in to weakness and asked Booth to cancel his lunch. She had felt braver then than she did now, with Mrs. Ingram's departure imminent.

Was the watcher watching, was the silent telephone building up for some dramatic outburst?

Be sensible, she admonished herself, don't lie around like a dying swan waiting for disaster. One could will disaster to happen, she had read somewhere, as accident-prone people did. Perhaps that was what she had been doing all this week. So why didn't she get out of the house, have a snack lunch at the crowded counter in the supermarket (where no one could do her any harm by staring at her) then shop until she called for Kitty? It was high time she completely replenished her larder, as Mrs. Ingram kept pointing out.

Fight down this nasty rising uneasiness. Just behave normally.

If that was something that was still

within her capacity.

Nothing went wrong with these simple plans, except that she found shopping difficult. She simply couldn't concentrate on such mundane things as cereals, greens, meat, fish. Max liked a roast for Sunday lunch, no matter how hot the weather. But it was as if Sunday didn't exist, as if they would never sit down to an ordinary Sunday lunch again. The whole weekend seemed to be lost in some sort of limbo. In the space of one week life had become too extraordinary.

Oranges and pears for a fruit salad, a lettuce and tomatoes, sliced ham and tongue, some smoked salmon for Max as a treat. He would want to celebrate tonight, most likely. Coffee and a sandwich at the lunch counter, and no one watching her. There were crowds of shoppers coming and going. She couldn't see everybody. Yet she had a certainty that today she was not being followed.

When she got in the car and drove slowly toward the school she saw no sign of a green Mini, no car hung on her tail.

Did this mean that her persecution was over?

Because Max had now achieved his ambition? Or because Mrs. Daphne Gibson had been found?

Let's not analyze things too much, let's not have these kinky thoughts. Let's just enjoy the reprieve and be gay with Kitty and Sam. She would give them a tea party in the garden. In spite of the heat she would make some of Sam's favorite hot scones with strawberry jam. The best way to please Kitty was to please her friends.

The children sensed her happier mood and giggled wildly over one of Sam's less funny jokes all the way home.

If they were going to be out in the sun, Ella said, Kitty must wear her cotton sunbonnet. She had a fine skin that burned too easily. Kitty demurred, but agreed when Sam said she looked smashing in it. She was pure female, that child. The absurd and touching thing was that the pair of them behaved exactly like a married couple. When Ella looked out of the window and saw them dragging the dolls' pram to the bottom of the garden she knew that they would be playing mothers and fathers for the rest of the afternoon.

The telephone remained blissfully silent, the police didn't come. Ella's feeling of reprieve lasted. She decided to put her feet up for half an hour before getting the children's tea. Then she would be fresh and cheerful for Max this evening, her debilitating tiredness of the last few days gone.

She couldn't forget the strange and frightening events of the week, but perhaps she could reduce their importance in her mind.

The children's voices lulled her. She didn't intend to fall asleep, and woke guiltily in what she imagined to be a few minutes.

The clock, however, told her that an hour and a half had gone by.

It was like the evening when she had lost two hours before going up to bed. The realization made her feel shaken and unreal, her earlier tranquillity ebbing away. She was late getting Kitty's and Sam's tea, and the house was much too quiet.

The garden was much too quiet, too. The

fact struck Ella as she went into the kitchen. The door was wide open, and she should have been able to hear Kitty's prattle clearly.

There wasn't a sound. Neither was there any sign of the children.

Ella flew outside. "Kitty!" she called. "Sam! Come along, you two. Where are you hiding?"

Actually, there was nowhere for them to hide except the tool shed, and that, she discovered, was empty. She stood in its doorway, opening and closing her hands in nervous tension, willing herself to think quietly.

They might have gone to Sam's place. But she knew they wouldn't have, because Kitty didn't care for Sam's mother, indeed was a little afraid of her. They might be playing in the street, which they knew was forbidden.

A hasty dash to the front gate showed the wide empty tree-lined street with nothing but a tradesman's van in the distance.

They were not in the house, she knew. They could never have been so silent.

Where's Kitty? That evil voice of

yesterday was ringing in her head.

Be calm, she told herself. Think. Don't rush to the telephone to bother Max, or the police. There must be a simple answer to this.

And there was, of course. It flashed into her mind a moment later. The dolls' pram had disappeared as well as the children. One simply couldn't imagine a kidnapper agreeing to kidnap eleven dolls in advanced stages of dilapidation as well as his human prey.

Ella found herself giggling weakly at the thought. She was remembering Kitty's maternal prattle yesterday to her dolls. *Your father will come tomorrow and take us for a walk. . . .*

So they had gone for their walk. And almost certainly their destination was the old house.

Comparatively reassured, although still alarmed at the thought of two such innocents straying so far, Ella hastily put on her flat walking shoes, pulled the door shut behind her, and was running down the garden and climbing over the stile into the long field.

She had vague hopes that she might see Sam's tawny head and Kitty's pink sunbonnet bobbing in the distance over the tops of the wild poppies and purple loosestrife. Like a Renoir painting.

But there was no sign of them. They had probably arrived at their destination while she still lay asleep in the darkened living room.

She kept running. She was thinking of the hot ashes on the hearth, and that tramp or hippie who might still be lurking. Or the owl screeching and scaring Kitty to death. Or Kitty trying to pick wild flowers and getting caught up in brambles.

Charming as it was, it was not an innocent garden. Somehow she had known that all along.

Drenched with perspiration, dizzy with breathlessness, Ella burst into the garden, then made herself stop in her wild flight to listen for the children's voices.

She had been so sure she would hear them.

But there was only the familiar drone of the bees, the whistling of birds, and the occasional harsh jagged cry of a crow. Not a human voice was to be heard.

Ella ran up the weedy path, calling, "Kitty! Kitty! Sam!"

A startled blackbird swooped from a holly bush. The big house drowsed in the hot afternoon sun.

"Kitty — " Ella began to call again, then stopped on a sharply indrawn breath. That patch of pink on the terrace steps. Kitty's sunbonnet! So they were here!

"Come out from where you're hiding, you naughty children!" she exclaimed, and waited for the burst of guilty giggles. When the silence continued, the slightest panic touched her voice. "I'm not angry, Kitty. Sam. I only want to find you."

The French doors into the ballroom were open an inch or so. Ella's spirits rose again. So they were indoors, hiding in a cupboard or under the stairs, the little wretches. Yes, there was the perambulator tipped on its side, and all the dolls spilled out onto the floor.

But that was odd. Disturbing. Kitty would never have gone off to play leaving her dolls in such an abandoned way. Neither would Sam, simply because, knowing Kitty, he would know better than to do so.

So wherever they were, they must have gone rather quickly. And not of their own free will?

Now Ella didn't attempt to repress her panic. She ran through the ground floor rooms, and up the stairs, calling for the children. She didn't hesitate to open closed doors, to look in cavernous cupboards. She had no time for personal fear.

But if the children had accidentally got locked in somewhere they would hear her calling, and answer.

So they couldn't be here.

Then why the abandoned dolls, the discarded sunbonnet?

Something had frightened them. Yes, that was it. They had dropped everything and fled. They would be halfway home by now.

But wouldn't she have met them on the way?

She made herself go around to the front, and search among the dismal diseased-looking laurels. The driveway was empty. She knew instinctively that Kitty would not have agreed to play in this part of the garden.

But wherever Kitty was now, she was not playing. Of that, Ella was fearfully sure.

"Kitty!" she called again. "Kitty, Kitty, Kitty!"

She thought she heard the far-off bubbling screech of the white owl. She wasn't sure. She was completely sure that there was no child's voice answering.

Acting on blind impulse she went back into the ballroom and bundled the dolls into the perambulator, and pulled it behind her. In the garden, she retrieved the pink sunbonnet.

When Kitty got home she would be deeply distressed if her dolls were not there. She would have to drag this forlorn family the two miles home, retarding her own pace, simply because it was necessary. It was the sort of thing even a mother paralyzed with fear would do for her child.

But of course she would find Kitty, and that beguiling wretch Sam, before she got home.

Don't be late for Kitty. . . . Don't forget Kitty. . . . Where's Kitty? . . . The voices screamed in her head.

Max — and someone else — had been

trying to tell her all the week that Kitty was in danger.

But why hadn't they spelled it out for her, letter by letter? The dazed state she had been in she hadn't paid enough attention. She had let herself fall asleep. And now Kitty was gone.

She made herself take time, when she reached home, to telephone Sam's mother on the slim chance of the children being there.

"I thought Sam went home with Kitty," said Sam's mother. "He always wants to. He's crazy about her, isn't he? Funny. Kids." She was a slow stupid woman. She hadn't noticed the panic in Ella's voice. "What's wrong Mrs. Simpson? Is Sam up to some prank?"

"I don't know, but I'm just on my way to the police. Both the children are missing, and I'm worried to death. I'm sorry to have to tell you this, but you ought to know."

"That boy! Don't get in a flap, Mrs. Simpson. He runs off twice a week. He'll turn up."

"Of course he will. But I'm going to the police all the same."

Chapter 14

Kidnapped. Ella didn't say the word. The serious young police sergeant did.

But he said it in a casual joking manner, perhaps to lessen her very obvious agitation. "How long have they been away, Mrs. Simpson? Two hours? They'll turn up. You don't imagine they're kidnapped, do you?"

"Kitty — my daughter — is blond and pretty. My husband has been saying lately to watch her, she'd be fair prey for one of those horrible rapists."

"What are the children's ages, Mrs. Simpson?"

"Kitty is six, Sam seven."

"And Sam's parents are whom?"

Ella clenched her hands in impatience.

"Can't I answer these questions later?

Can't you put out a call now? I'm so afraid something's happened to them in that old house."

"What old house, Mrs. Simpson?"

"The one across the fields from our house. It's scheduled for demolition. You see, Kitty would never run away leaving her dolls unless she was made to. The dolls were all over the ballroom floor." She caught the sergeant's calm gaze, and said angrily, "I am *not* mad. I did *not* imagine this. It's all there if you want to go and see. The fireplace where there was a fire, the room where the owl screeched and Kitty and I thought it was a woman, the trampled grass in the garden. I wonder you've never found it."

The sergeant had leaned forward, his light-blue eyes intent.

"And when did you discover this house?"

"Last Sunday. Kitty and I had gone for a walk in the afternoon. Kitty and Sam wanted to go back again but I wouldn't let them. So they disappeared this afternoon when I was asleep. I know they were there because of the dolls, and Kitty's sunbonnet."

"I see," said the sergeant, rising. "Excuse me while I put out a call."

"Can I ring my husband?"

"By all means. I'll send policewoman Carter to you."

A brisk pretty young policewoman came and escorted Ella to a telephone. She had no qualms about interrupting Max even if he were closeted with the chairman himself.

When his secretary answered, Ella said urgently, "Penny, is my husband there?"

"I'm expecting him any minute. He's — "

"For God's sake, find him. It's terribly important."

"Is it?" By the note in Penny's voice Ella knew that she, too, had been infected by the general skepticism about poor Mrs. Simpson. "Wait a minute. I'll try."

An endless wait, while policewoman Carter, across the table, made notes about something on a pad. Then at last Max's voice, irritable, but with a not quite repressed triumph.

"Ella! You chose an awkward time. The boss was just telling me — "

"Max, Kitty's missing! We think she's kidnapped."

"Oh, my God!" There was genuine shock in Max's voice. Then rapidly, "Ella, is this fact? Or are you being hysterical again? Who is we?"

Ella was abruptly conscious of a cold strong anger overriding even her desperate fear.

"No, I am not being hysterical, Max. I am sitting here in the police station. A call has been put out to police cars to look for Kitty and Sam."

"Sam, too!" Now Max's voice sounded numb, as if he did believe her.

"They went to the old house. Kitty took her dolls. They've disappeared from there. Max, you've got to come home."

"I will. Right away." There was the shortest pause. "Ella, what have you told the police?"

"Everything, of course."

"And about your confused mental state, I hope," he said sharply, cruelly. Then, incredibly, his voice brightened. "Well, it probably doesn't matter now, because I've got the job."

Kitty was missing, and he was still harping on his precious job!

"Oh, to hell with the job," she cried furiously. "I'm sick of the sound of it."

The sergeant with the cold eyes, accompanied by a detective inspector, came back. They assured Ella that a search was already under way. She would have her daughter home in no time at all. But in the meantime perhaps she would answer a few questions. That old house, for instance. When she had first found it had she noticed anything significant about it? A scream that she had thought was an owl? That was interesting. And why hadn't she mentioned the house when they had made inquiries about the gray Jaguar and about her movements last Sunday afternoon? Why had her husband told her not to talk about it? Did she share his conviction that she suffered from fancies and hallucinations? Did she really think a sick wife would prejudice his appointment to this new job? Had she ever suspected that there might be a deeper reason for his urging her silence? Was Mrs. Daphne Gibson a close friend, or an acquaintance of her husband's? Hadn't she thought it might have been wise to report those persistent telephone calls, and her suspicion that she was being watched by a man or men in a green Mini car? Had she noticed the number of the Mini?

A cup of strong sweet tea was put in front of her. Ella took a sip and choked on it. She had no qualms about disobeying Max and pouring out all the complex events of the week to the police. She should have done so at the beginning. If she had, Kitty might not now be missing.

They took her home at last, and half an hour afterward Max arrived. He had got one of his colleagues to drive him from London. They swept into the driveway in a Jensen. Rich cars, Ella thought vaguely. The gray Jaguar, the new Rover, and now this impressive vehicle. A man in a modest green Mini would be ashamed to lurk about here.

Max's face was so grim that Ella knew he feared the worst. He tried to relieve his anxiety (or his guilt) by striking out at her.

"How did you come to let Kitty out of

your sight, Ella? Haven't I kept warning you lately?"

"She and Sam went to the old house, Max. I had fallen asleep and I didn't see them go."

He flinched distinctly.

"That damned house!" he exclaimed.

"Perhaps you would like to tell us what you know about that house, Mr. Simpson," the police sergeant said.

"I don't know anything. I've never been there. I've only listened to my wife who has some sort of hangup about it. Surely we're not going to talk about a house while these children are missing. Why aren't we all out looking for them? What's been done, may I ask?"

"Everything possible, I assure you, Mr. Simpson. We have men and cars and dogs out."

Ella noticed that the sergeant didn't add that his men had already searched this house from top to bottom, as if they expected to find Kitty and Sam smothered in a wardrobe. They had done it as tactfully and politely as possible, but it had been a terrible thing to endure. Especially since

308

Sam's mother was there, too, and had kept looking at Ella sideways as if she could easily believe that silly Mrs. Simpson might be absentminded enough or ghoulish enough to lock two children in a cupboard.

The sergeant then asked Max if he could clear up one or two points about the telephone calls. "The ones your wife says she's been having. You know about them, of course?"

"Only what my wife told me. And as you have probably realized, sergeant, she's been quite a sick woman. She's a bit muddled and absentminded. Frankly I didn't pay too much attention to her taller stories."

"But you also had these calls yourself, I believe? In the evening?"

"Oh, those, yes. From a business colleague. I was having a spot of bother — do I need to go into this now?"

Ella, hearing the familiar glibness in Max's voice, moved out of earshot. She couldn't stand any more of that.

Kitty! Where was Kitty? Don't be too frightened, my darling. We'll rescue you. . . .

Then Booth returned, and seeing the

police car, came bursting in to find out what was wrong. Hard on his heels, his sister Lorna was there, and immediately and predictably put on the kettle for cups of tea all around. Life in the suburbs was becoming just too exciting.

The living room was full of people, the nice policewoman, the sergeant, Max who couldn't sit still but kept prowling about twitching his fingers, Sam's mother, an aggressive redhead, and Booth and Lorna Bramwell.

Vaguely Ella knew that police investigations were going on at the old house, innocent Edith's house which had become so sinister. She gathered that they now thought it was where Mrs. Daphne Gibson had first been held captive and then murdered.

("Could the scream you heard, Mrs. Simpson, have been not an owl at all, but a woman?")

If this were true it would have been there that her clothes had been removed and subsequently burned (and the ashes buried at the end of that trail of bruised grass in the garden?). Only her naked body must have been taken away for disposal.

But all this horror was only an undercurrent in Ella's mind since she was entirely absorbed with anxiety for Kitty.

She did have a flash of panic when the sergeant said he would like Max to come down to the station to make a statement.

"But you haven't done anything, have you?" she asked. "Have you, Max?"

"Of course I haven't," Max said angrily. With a great effort he smoothed his face and assumed his persuasive honest earnest salesman's expression. "Ella, love, I'll tell you all about it later. I'm absolutely innocent, I assure you. I've never set eyes on Mrs. Daphne Gibson in my life."

Lorna, helped by the policewoman, made more tea. Booth sat beside Ella and held her hand. He didn't say much. Indeed he had scarcely said anything except, "I shouldn't have left you today," as if he were more responsible for her than her own husband. His serious face was creased with worry and remorse.

This ugly room, Ella thought. *I'll be glad to leave it.* The sun lying low over the neat garden. That, too, she was never going to miss.

"Did my husband have something to do with Mrs. Gibson's kidnapping?" she asked a little later, when it seemed that Max's last astonishing words had just penetrated her mind.

"Surely not," Booth said. "But it does seem as if he's been sitting on some vital information."

"I don't really care," said Ella wearily. "I only want Kitty safely home."

"That Sam!" declared Sam's mother. "He's the most disobedient child who ever lived. Mark my words, Mrs. Simpson, it'll be him who's led your Kitty astray. On the other hand, he's pretty sharp at getting out of trouble. And he doesn't like the dark. You'll see, they'll be home before dark."

Kitty didn't like the dark either. She had had a nightlight until she was four years old. Then her father said she had to stop being a baby. So Ella left the light on on the landing instead.

It must have been something very frightening that had happened this afternoon to make her abandon her family.

One would have to treat her very gently or she would have traumas afterward.

It was still daylight, but the shadows had lengthened. It was even a little cooler. At least something was making Ella give intermittent shivers.

Kitty and Sam wouldn't just have fled from the white owl's scream. So what had it been?

Booth's arm tightened around Ella. She didn't remember when he had put it there.

"At least it's a warm night if they have to sleep outdoors," said Sam's mother.

But they wouldn't be outdoors, they would be in that green Mini, held out of sight on the floor, and speeding off — to where?

"Oh, God, I can't stand it!" Ella burst out. "All the week Max has been telling me I'm mad. Now I wish I were, so I couldn't realize — couldn't think about — "

"You have a good cry, love," said the policewoman, emptying Ella's untouched cup of tea and refilling it with a strong hot brew that had the color if not the taste of poison.

"I kept thinking I'd be interfering too

313

much if I went to the police," Booth said. "I was alarmed but not alarmed enough. One gets accustomed to crimes or threats of crime, one accepts them. Ignores them. It's wrong. I play with words and do nothing."

"None of this is your fault," Ella said. It was necessary to make the effort to reassure this nice man. She made herself sip the nauseating tea. "Mr. Brontë," she murmured affectionately. She felt oddly drunk. "Words are your stock in trade."

She got up to walk to the open French windows as she had done repeatedly in the last two hours, to look across the hazy fields toward the clump of trees and the indistinct chimneys of Edith's house. The strange doomed place was still pulling her. Why was she being kept here? Why wasn't she allowed to go out and search the fields, the hedgerows, the dark shrubbery leading to the house?

That's all being attended to, Mrs. Simpson. You must rest, Mrs. Simpson. You must be here for the children's return. There are some more questions we would like you to answer, Mrs. Simpson. Have some more tea, Mrs. Simpson. Drown in hot sweet tea, and who cares. . . .

"Mummy!" whispered Kitty.

Ella's breath held.

"Why are all those people here, Mummy? *Mummy!* We've been here ages. Sam won't come in while all those people are here."

She thought it was the voices in her head again. They were coming out of the empty air now instead of through the medium of the telephone.

"Mumm-ee!"

She listened intently and tried a tentative word. "Kitty?"

"I'm *here,* Mummy."

Kitty's blond head, unfamiliarly tousled like an untidy haystack, appeared cautiously from behind the heavy green syringa bush that grew at the side of the window. She had been crying, but some time ago, for her tears had dried in dusty streaks. Her look of acute apprehension and misery gave Ella the necessary shock to bring her to life.

"Kitty!" she shrieked, and dragged the dusty little apparition out of its hiding place, unable to believe that it was real. "Kitty, my darling, my love!"

Kitty wriggled impatiently in the crushing embrace.

"Call Sam, Mummy. He's scared to come in."

"Sam scared! To come in here! That's funny. Listen, everybody!" Unbelievably, Ella was laughing. She couldn't help it. She was glowing with joy and renewed life. "Sam's scared of something! He's scared of us!"

Sam's mother came hurrying out.

"Sam, you little devil, where are you hiding?"

Furtively Sam's head appeared from behind Max's treasured clump of perennial phlox, just about to come into bloom.

"Come on, Sam," said Ella gently. "We're not cross."

"Aren't we, though," said Sam's mother, tightening lips that might have trembled. "After that fright you've given us, my lad — "

"I think they need long cold drinks," said Lorna Bramwell briskly. "They look as if they'd crossed the Sahara."

"Ask them what happened," said the policewoman in a low voice in Ella's ear.

"Don't push them. Just quietly."

Sam, hanging his head, as dilapidated a figure as one of Kitty's dolls, stood on the patio muttering that it was all his fault because he had forgotten to take his gun.

"When we heard someone walking about upstairs we just had to run. We left the family and Kitty cried."

He had cried himself, by the look of his smudged face.

"Who was walking about?" Ella asked.

"Kitty said it was Edith's father. She had a cross father. But he died hundreds of years ago, so it must have been a ghost. And I hadn't got my gun."

"Guns are no good for ghosts," said Ella. "You were very wise to run away."

"We hid in a ditch with nettles," said Kitty, outraged.

"I said we ought to stay there till dark, but Kitty wanted to come home, so we risked it." Sam's assurance was returning. "Why are the police here, Mrs. Simpson?"

"They're looking for you. Don't you realize the trouble you've caused?" Sam eyed his mother respectfully, then his eyes began to gleam, his chin got its familiar cocky tilt.

"Gee, Mum, are you telling the truth? They've got a search on for Kitty and me!"

"And don't be proud of it! Come here. Give me a kiss. I don't mind your mucky face. You're a caution. Your father will be having a word with you. You'd better promise never to go off like that again."

"I have to go once more, Mum, to get Kitty's family. I'll go in the morning. I promised Kitty I'd get the family back. This time I'll take my gun."

"Well, there's a surprise for you both," said Ella. "The family's safe and sound in the kitchen. I brought them home myself."

Everyone had said, But you didn't stop to drag that thing home, Mrs. Simpson? When you were so worried and in such a hurry? But why? Are you sure you're telling us the truth about everything?

Here was the answer for everyone to see, in Kitty's suddenly transformed and sparkling face.

Kitty had lost her children, too, she also had been suffering from anxiety and deprivation.

To love children one had to understand them. Max doesn't. He doesn't try or he hasn't time. From the moment I knew he didn't care about the baby I knew a lot of other things.

I suppose I have been acting a little oddly lately, even without these traumatic events. It's quite something to discover that the man you married six years ago could be — is — someone else altogether.

Chapter 15

Everyone had gone and Kitty was in bed and asleep when Max came back. He looked chastened, an unfamiliar look for Max, and one that scarcely went with the objects he carried, a bottle of champagne, a dozen red roses, and a long package that he said was a doll for Kitty. It was time that she had a decent doll. Those shameful caricatures she carted about must make people think he and Ella were unnatural parents. The roses were for Ella.

Didn't Max know yet that Kitty loved her shabby caricatures, and Ella her wild flowers?

"They told me Kitty was home and undamaged," Max said. "That little brat Sam. I'll bet he was responsible."

"What's the champagne for?" Ella asked.

"We have a celebration. Don't you realize you're now in the presence of the new six-thousand-a-year export manager of a great textile company? And you don't know the rest of it. All being well, I'm to be elected to the board at the end of the year. So we've got to crack a bottle of champagne to that." He looked at her expectantly. "Ella? Say something."

His jubilation was brittle, however. Ella could see the uneasiness in his eyes, his slightly hangdog air.

"Congratulations, Max. But what happened at the police station?"

"You're more interested in that than my future, aren't you?"

"After what I've gone through, frankly, yes." She laid the roses on the table. "These won't last a day in this weather."

"I was trying to make up for being beastly about you picking my flowers."

My flowers, my car, my wife, my child. . . . Extensions of the successful Mr. Max Simpson.

"You did tell me I could pick them."

"I know I did." It was so unlike him to admit a lie or a failure that Ella knew he had something serious to tell her. "I can explain it all. Teasing you like that was something I had to do."

"Had to do!" Ella looked at him in astonishment. "And I would use a rather stronger word than teasing," she added. "I would say torturing."

"Oh, no, come off it, Ella. It wasn't that bad. I only had to throw doubts on your credibility. Doing things like putting the clock on that night to make you think you'd lost two hours, rattling the letter box to scare you, all those silly things that were effective because it was only your word against mine. I hated seeing you so puzzled. You were such easy material, it was taking candy from a child. It was hell. Believe me, it was just as bad for me as for you. But I had to do it."

Ella had backed away from him. The enormity of it was just beginning to sink in.

"So I really was being brainwashed!" she said. "And by my own husband." Her voice rose incredulously. "Deliberately."

"I couldn't help it, Ella. What you didn't know was that I was being blackmailed by those two young thugs. It would have been highly dangerous not to do what they told me to. Dealing with them was like dealing with dynamite. Look, couldn't we have the champagne before we talk any more?"

"I don't think so. I think you must tell me everything now." Ella felt a chair behind her and sat down. "The young thugs, of course, were the men in the Mini watching me. One of them had the chore of following me. The other rang me up and said those frightening things. And you knew all the time who they were and what they were doing."

"I didn't say I knew who they were. I don't even now. I only know that before I'd left the police station they'd been picked up in that green Mini and brought in for questioning. Actually the police had already been suspicious about their behavior."

"What are they to be charged with?"

"Kidnapping."

"Mrs. Daphne Gibson," Ella said, unsurprised.

"That's right. They're young dropout students, both on drugs. They've got nasty clever perverted minds, and if I could lay my hands on them again — "

"Again!"

"I have been at their mercy once, I might tell you, with a gun stuck in my ribs."

"Max!"

Mistaking her shock for horrified sympathy, Max said self-pityingly, "You didn't know, you see. I had to shut up about it, pretend it was only a business colleague I had gone out to see."

"The man who rang last Sunday evening! You said it was O'Brien."

"That was just a name I made up. It was these two crooks. They made some nasty threats over the telephone, then asked me to meet them in their green Mini at the corner of the park. They wore dark glasses and stocking masks. They made me get in the car, and then drove around until they'd made their bargain."

"What bargain?" Ella cried.

"They'd found out where I worked and they knew I'd just come back from abroad. They got it out of me that I was up for promotion, and they said they'd spread the rumor that I regularly smuggled watches and other things after my trips. It would be their word against mine, but it would be a pretty bad smear. They said they could ruin my job."

"Could they?" Ella asked. "Have you really smuggled things, then? That mink jacket?"

"There never was a mink jacket. But" — Max's eyes fell — "About a year ago I did smuggle in a rather expensive camera. It was crazy of me. I wanted it for a colleague." He saw Ella wince and added defensively, "Someone I owed something to."

"A bribe?"

"No!"

"Someone who could use influence to help you in your career?"

"I suppose so."

"You shouldn't have spoiled the gesture by a bit of meanness like dodging customs duty," Ella said tiredly.

"Oh, you! It's that crazy honesty of yours that's been the trouble. If it hadn't been for that, I'd have told you all this at the beginning and asked you to cooperate. But I know you too well. You'd have been off to the police like a shot. Even if you knew Kitty might disappear."

"Kitty! You're telling me you let those monsters threaten you with that, and still you didn't go to the police!"

"How could I? You haven't heard it all yet. These men were desperate. They were kidnappers and murderers, too, although I didn't know that at the time. You certainly must know now that they murdered Mrs. Gibson in that old house."

"Oh, God!" Ella went very pale, remembering the bubbling scream from the attic room, then the lovely floating flight of the disturbed owl. "Kitty and I had been there that very afternoon."

"Exactly. That's the root of the matter. They didn't know how much you had heard. Or seen. One of them followed you home to find out where you lived."

The cracking of twigs in the dark shrubbery, the imagined footsteps behind the hawthorn hedge, the uncanny feeling of being followed. . . .

"And to find out who we were," Ella said. "Max, how awful!"

"That's what I've been telling you."

"They thought I might tell the police something suspicious, so my story must be discredited. I must be proved to be — "

"A bit loony," said Max deprecatingly.

"Mad."

"Not mad, love. Just the things I said you were. Fanciful, absentminded."

"Worse than that." Ella's voice was bleak.

"Well. Maybe I overdid it a bit. It was only to be for two or three days until they collected the ransom money and disappeared." Max gave a short laugh, half-admiring. "They damn nearly succeeded, too. Their scheme was so amateur that they almost got away with it. Except that they were scared off by a pair of lovers. So they kept me on the hook another day while they tried again. But in the meantime Mrs. Gibson's body was found."

"Clumsy!" Ella cried intensely. "Clumsy!"

"Well, they're half around the bend with drugs. Living in a fantasy world."

"Like your poor wife."

"Now, love — "

"I didn't mean they were clumsy, I meant you were."

"I had to be. I've just been explaining it

to you. I really thought that if it was only for two or three days we could survive. Don't look like that, Ella. What else could I have done? Have them blabbing all those lies to my boss at this critical stage?"

"So you risked destroying me instead."

"Now that's being pretty melodramatic."

"But you actually took that risk, Max. I really do find that appalling."

"Ella, I've just explained. If you had been a different sort of person, I might have told you about it at the beginning and asked you to cooperate. But you know how compulsively honest you are. You'd have been off to the police like a shot. I couldn't have trusted you. Really. But it's all over now. And look at us, we're not in too bad shape. I admit that hospital thing yesterday was a shocker, but we'll be none the worse in a day or two. At least we're alive, which is something. Mrs. Daphne Gibson isn't. Think of her for a change."

It was a long time before Ella spoke again.

"So what's to happen to you?"

"Darling, don't you take anything in? I've got the job. Right now we're going to split a bottle of champagne. As soon as I've found my feet we'll look for a new house, get out of this neighborhood."

"I meant what was going to happen to you with the police. Aren't you now an accessory after the fact, or whatever you call it?"

Max looked momentarily uncomfortable.

"They've told me not to go away. Not to go abroad, I mean. They know I was being blackmailed in a particularly nasty way. I think you'll find I get plenty of sympathy."

"Will you?"

"You don't sound as if you believe that."

"I was just wondering who would be listening to my side of the story."

"Oh, Ella! I've told you I'm sorry. I loathed doing it. But what else could I do?"

Ella shrugged.

"Indeed, what else could the new export manager of Fabritex do? So now I'm to be certified as sane, after all."

"Oh, God, Ella. Don't take it like that."

"Supposing I had really gone out of my mind. Brainwashing is dangerous."

"Not over such a short time!"

"No? Not when you knew I was already

tired and shaken and sad after the baby. Women in that state, you kept saying."

"Then just forgive me. Ella, darling! Let's take the champagne up to bed."

She stared at him. She shouldn't be so surprised since she knew now that he had never understood her. Or wanted to. I would have taken too much valuable time from his job and his ambitions. This country needed young keen ruthless driving men like this, sending out the goods, bringing back the cash. The new empire builders. The disciples of the new religion.

"Have you ever thought that the intriguing art of brainwashing could become addictive?" she said quite mildly. "No, you go to bed, Max. I'll stay down here for a while. Oh, and by the way, I promised Mother I'd bring Kitty down this weekend."

"Tomorrow!" Max said, outraged. "But we were going to try out the new car. I was going to drive you to — no, I don't suppose we can go to that old house now. The police will be fingerprinting it. Finding your prints, too, you foolish — Never mind. But don't go this weekend, Ella."

"I must. It's the heat. I must get into the country. Breathe pure air."

"For heaven's sake, don't get as eccentric as your mother."

Ella gave a wide cool smile.

"Perhaps I'm eccentric already. Perhaps you've been right all this week, after all."

He gave an impatient exclamation.

"Now don't start getting cryptic. When will you be back? Sunday evening or Monday morning?"

Never, said Ella to herself. But let's break the news calmly, civilly, when we're in a more balanced state of mind. "Go to bed, Max," she said. "Get some sleep."

Poor Max. He couldn't understand why she wouldn't allow him to take them to the station in the morning, or why Kitty left her new doll at home and traveled with her old ones packed carefully in a wicker basket with a rug over them.

They got into a taxi and Ella waved to his good-looking figure, so attractive physically, so sterile mentally, and now suddenly so lonely as he stood in the doorway. She knew she would never voluntarily see him again.

But as the train pulled out of the station, and Kitty busied herself arranging her dolls comfortably on the empty seat beside them, she allowed herself a small smile. Of hope? No, perhaps more of faith. Not all men got their priorities as wrong as Max did. Some had honest enduring qualities. Take Booth Bramwell, for instance.

Courtesy, and a very real sense of friendship, had made her take ten minutes to rush in next door to say good-bye to Lorna and Booth.

Lorna, hearing of Ella's departure, had said a friendly good-bye, and then had excused herself to go into the kitchen to attend to some urgent cooking. Booth had rumpled his hair, and said, in a tentative way, "Where will you be living, Ella?"

Not "When will you be back?" but "Where will you be living?" That was perceptive. He was a very perceptive man.

"In the meantime with my parents. In Peasford, Dorset. It's a very pretty village — "

"I might come down sometime."

"Might you? Do you like villages? Perhaps later, sometime." Her voice was vague. Then, seeing his wary eyes and realizing he was as suspicious of hope as she was, she made an effort. "You'll be very welcome. In the meantime, comfort Sam. Don't let him think Kitty's a fickle female."

"Sam and I," said Booth rather more firmly, "might go into partnership and come down together."

"Might you?" Ella's voice was still vague, but suddenly her vivid and unpredictable imagination was seeing Kitty's radiant face as the two stepped out of the car in front of the old ivy-covered many-chimneyed house.

She realized that she would enjoy showing her friend Mr. Brontë her childhood home. She remembered their compatibility in Edith's house.

Compatibility was a good word. A really sound and satisfying word.